Ultimate
Collector's Guide

by Meredith Rusu

SCHOLASTIC INC.

Published by Scholastic Inc., *Publishers since 1920*. SCHOLASTIC and associated logos are trademarks and/or registered trademarks of Scholastic Inc.

The publisher does not have any control over and does not assume any responsibility for author or third-party websites or their content.

ISBN 978-1-338-25617-8

10 9 8 7 6 5 4 3   18 19 20 21 22

Printed in the U.S.A.   40
First printing 2018

Book design by Becky James

Contents

Did you know Beanie Boos come in five different sizes?

R Regular

M Medium

L Large

EL Extra-Large

C Clip

Welcome to the World of BEANIE BOOS™

They're cute. They're cuddly. They have big eyes, even bigger hearts, and they can't wait to meet YOU!

Welcome to the world of Beanie Boos! These adorable animals are bursting with personality, and there's a special friend for everyone.

In this book, you'll discover fun facts, silly poems, and much, much more about all your favorite Boos. From Rainbow the poodle and Flippy the fish to Kacey the koala and even Izzy the ladybug, there are so many to choose. That's why everyone loves the Beanie Boos!

The World of Beanie Boos

The Beanie Boos' world is full of beauty, wonder, and even a little magic. Check out the different places where you're sure to spot your favorite Boos!

FANTASTICAL FOREST Deep in the Fantastical Forest, the leaves shimmer and shine like crystal. Some of the most magical Beanie Boos live here, tucked away in hidden nooks and crannies.

AWESOME ARCTIC The coolest Beanie Boos spend their days slipping and sliding on the ice and snow of the Awesome Arctic. It's a true winter wonderland!

JAZZY JUNGLE There's always a party going on in the Jazzy Jungle. From tree climbing to vine swinging to river hopping, there's no stopping these bold and brave Boos!

OUTRAGEOUS OCEAN These friendly Beanie Boos will always leap out of the waves to say hello! That is, if they aren't too busy playing hide-and-seek in the coral reefs.

MYSTIC MOUNTAINS The Mystic Mountains are filled with snowy peaks and quiet magic. Thoughtful and wise Beanie Boos live here, along with some playful friends.

MARVELOUS METROPOLIS With bustling bakeries, shops, theaters, and restaurants, the Marvelous Metropolis is home to the most cultured and stylish Beanie Boos.

IRIDESCENT ISLANDS Sunny days and warm weather make the Iridescent Islands just perfect for Beanie Boos to kick back, relax, and soak up the tropical lifestyle.

FABULOUS FARM The Fabulous Farm is busy, busy, busy! Beanie Boos here are typically hard at work, but they always make time for their friends and a slice of apple pie.

FRIENDLY FIELD Green pastures and colorful flowers stretch for miles in the Friendly Field. Beanie Boos romp and play, popping up from the tall grass to laugh and invent new games.

SHIMMERING SKY The white, puffy clouds in the Shimmering Sky are the place many winged Beanie Boos call home. They spend their days chasing stars and sliding down rainbows.

SUNNY SAVANNAH It's hot and sunny out on the savannah—just the way the Boos who live here like it! Every day is a safari adventure roaming the plains and plateaus.

Turn the page for
awesome fun—
Meet the Beanie Boos
one by one!

Alpine

This adorable little reindeer lives way up north above the Arctic Circle. He loves to romp in the snow, and his biggest dream is to join Santa's sleigh team!

PERSONALITY: Spunky

FAVORITE FOOD OR DRINK: Hot cocoa

LOVES: Fresh-fallen snow

SECRET TALENT: Building snowball castles

FAVORITE COLOR: Winter white

FAVORITE HOLIDAY: Christmas

PERSONAL POEM:
At last, it's that time of year
For holiday spirit to reappear!

BIRTHDAY: December 21

All About Me!

Alpine has a festive holiday look, too!

10

Anabelle

PERSONALITY: Cute and cuddly

FAVORITE FOOD OR DRINK:
Malted milkshakes

LOVES: Getting her paws
on a new book

MOST STRIKING FEATURE:
Twinkling eyes

ENJOYS: Stories with happy endings

FAVORITE BOOK: *Puss in Boots*

PERSONAL POEM:
I like to read riddles and rhymes
And long tales of magical times.

BIRTHDAY:
October 1

Anabelle is a sweet kitty who adores
reading. Fairy tales are her favorite, and
she can usually be found curled up high on
the shelves of the library with a good book.

Anora

PERSONALITY: Warmhearted

FAVORITE FOOD OR DRINK:
Dragon fruit

LOVES: Spending time with friends

KNOWN FOR:
Her famous loop-de-loop flying
move

MOTTO: Dream on!

PERSONAL POEM:
I'm lucky to have a friend like you.
You make all my dreams come true.

BIRTHDAY:
August 28

Anora lives in the Fantastical Forest,
where her favorite hobby is soaring high
above the trees, practicing fancy flying
tricks. She dreams of flying in the Beanie
Boolympics one day.

Aqua

PERSONALITY: Bubbly

FAVORITE FOOD OR DRINK: Bubble tea

LOVES: A good gabfest

HANGS OUT WITH: Her schoolmates

BEST FRIEND: Flippy the Fish

PERSONAL POEM:
When I'm in the reef, I'm a
    happy fish.
And playing all day is my only wish!

BIRTHDAY: February 18

Chat, chat, chat. Aqua can't stop chitchatting! This feisty fish loves telling stories, and when she gets going, she can make quite the bubble storm underwater!

Aria

RMLC
Fantastical Forest
Animal:
Owl

PERSONALITY: Vibrant

FAVORITE FOOD: Lollipops

LOVES: Musicals

KNOWN FOR: Sliding down rainbows

FAVORITE SONG: "Owl Always Love You"

SPECIAL TALENT:
Winging it on karaoke night

PERSONAL POEM:
You can't miss me when I take flight
Because my colors are bold and
    bright!

BIRTHDAY:
November 15

Aria is a rainbow-colored owl who can't help stealing the spotlight. While most owls hoot during the night, Aria soars during the daytime, singing her favorite songs.

Arsenity

Mystic Mountains
Animal: Sheep
R

PERSONALITY: Quiet and wise

FAVORITE FOOD OR DRINK: Noodles

LOVES: The fresh mountain air

LUCKY COLOR: Purple

SECRET HOBBY: Knitting

PERSONAL POEM:
One more reason for you to keep:
In 2015 it is the year of the sheep.

BIRTHDAY: February 18

This woolly little sheep lives high in the Mystic Mountains. He's soft-spoken but strong and is known to bring good fortune to his friends.

Asia

Mystic Mountains
Animal: Tiger
RMLC

PERSONALITY: Cheerful

FAVORITE FOOD OR DRINK: Strawberry ice cream

LOVES: The mountain sunset

MOTTO: Think pink!

DISTANT RELATIVE: The Pink Panther

PERSONAL POEM:
Just call my name
    and I'll come in a wink.
Then you'll see my white fur and
    my eyes that are pink!

BIRTHDAY: June 6

Asia is a striped tiger who can't get enough of the color pink. Pink crayons, pink flowers, pink cotton candy—her friends even say she has a heart of pink gold!

Austin

PERSONALITY: Go-getter

FAVORITE FOOD OR DRINK:
Woofles with syrup

LOVES: Full moons

ALWAYS: On the go

CARRIES: His Paw-Pad Scheduler

DOESN'T BELIEVE IN: Being
fashionably late

PERSONAL POEM:
Woof is mostly what I say
And at the park is where I play!

BIRTHDAY:
May 30

This city dog doesn't let the grass grow under his paws. He's out and about every day of the week, checking out what's new in town, playing fetch at the park, and even leading his monthly Bark at the Mail Carrier Club.

Avril

R
Fantastical Forest
Animal:
Rabbit

PERSONALITY: Chipper

FAVORITE FOOD OR DRINK:
Carrots

LOVES: Gardening

TALENT: Baking carrot cake

ENJOYS: Spring showers

FAVORITE HOLIDAY: Easter

PERSONAL POEM:
Going hippity hoppity is
   what I can do
And nibbling on carrots
   is lots of fun, too!

BIRTHDAY: May 12

Avril is very proud of her vegetable garden: It's where she grows all her tasty carrots! She bakes special treats using her homegrown veggies and is famous for her Custard Carrot Cake.

Babs

R
Marvelous
Metropolis
Animal:
Lamb

PERSONALITY: Sprightly

FAVORITE FOOD OR DRINK:
Spinach salad

LOVES: Window-shopping

ADORES: Attending shop openings with friends

FAVORITE GAME: Skipping rope

SECRET WISH: To buy everything she sees!

PERSONAL POEM:
I love to run and jump and play
So we'll have fun all through the day!

BIRTHDAY: April 21

All About Me!

Babs is a starry-eyed lamb with a love of window-shopping. She makes a game out of skipping through town and guessing what new surprises the shops have in store.

15

Bamboo

RMC
Mystic Mountains
Animal:
Panda

PERSONALITY: Hungry

FAVORITE FOOD OR DRINK: Bamboo biscuits

LOVES: Munching

SECRET WISH: To become a competitive eater

DISLIKES: Slippery slopes

MOTTO: Is it lunchtime yet?

PERSONAL POEM:
I love to crunch bamboo when I eat.
But I ate so much, I can't see
my feet!

BIRTHDAY: June 7

Bamboo may have gone overboard with munching on snacks. All that food has made him quite . . . round. So round, in fact, he keeps accidentally rolling down the mountain!

Barley

R
Marvelous
Metropolis
Animal:
Dog

PERSONALITY: Rebellious

FAVORITE FOOD OR DRINK: Maple syrup

LOVES: Writing songs

FAVORITE BAND: Bone Jovi

DREAM: Being the lead singer in his own fur band

SECRET: He loves when people pet him.

PERSONAL POEM:
I have a cute and fluffy face.
Please take me home, that's the
right place.

BIRTHDAY: August 24

Barley's father owns the Bushy Barber Salon, so everyone thought Barley would follow in his dad's paw prints. But not Barley! He's a rebel who keeps his fur long and dreams of making it big as a singer.

Baron

PERSONALITY: Mysterious

FAVORITE FOOD OR DRINK:
Cherry juice

LOVES: Nighttime

FAVORITE SPOT:
The shadows

DISLIKES: Full
moons

HOME: A dark
cave in the
Fantastical Forest

PERSONAL POEM:
I fly around all through the night
And during the day I'm out of sight!

BIRTHDAY: October 5

All About Me!

Baron is dark and mysterious, flitting through
the night and sticking close to the shadows. If
you hear a strange flapping sound behind you,
watch out! Baron likes to bite everything in
sight!

Beaks

Beaks the toucan *loves* fruit. Fruity drinks, fruit salad—he's even colored his beak to match his favorite fruity treats! You can usually find him high in the island trees, nibbling on peaches and pineapples.

PERSONALITY: Perky

FAVORITE FOOD OR DRINK:
Any type of fruit

LOVES: Making smoothies

DREAM: To open his own juice bar

MOTTO: Everything is tooty-fruity!

SECRET TALENT: Tossing berries in the air and catching them in his beak

PERSONAL POEM:
Fruit is my favorite food to eat.
I even like it more than meat!

BIRTHDAY: November 16

All About Me!

Bloom

PERSONALITY: Flowery

FAVORITE FOOD OR DRINK:
Honeysuckle pie

LOVES: Sniffing flowers

SIGNATURE PERFUME SCENT:
Lovely lilac

DREAM: Opening a perfume shop
in Paris

HER FRIENDS SAY: Bloom is just
blooming with ideas!

PERSONAL POEM:
Of all the things
    I do in spring,
Hopping round's
    my favorite thing!

BIRTHDAY:
April 18

Bloom lives in her very own flower garden filled
with petunias, lilies, and lavender. She makes
perfume from the flowers she grows and
gives it to her friends!

Blossom

PERSONALITY: Wide-eyed

FAVORITE FOOD OR DRINK: Milk

LOVES: When her mama sings her
a lullaby

FAVORITE THING: Her pink-and-
green blankie

ENJOYS: Nighttime cuddles

FAVORITE NURSERY RHYME:
"Mary Had a Little Lamb"

PERSONAL POEM:
Pinks and greens are in my fur.
Springtime colors are best for sure!

BIRTHDAY:
April 10

Blossom is a baby lamb born in the spring.
She has so much to discover in the great,
wide world! For now, she's sticking close
to her mama and taking baby steps.

Blueberry

PERSONALITY: Nutty

FAVORITE FOOD OR DRINK:
Macadamia nuts

LOVES: Climbing high in the trees

SECRET TALENT: Making collages
out of nut shells

DISLIKES: Fruit salad

HOBBY: Whipping
up batches of nut butter

PERSONAL POEM:
Blueberry is a treetop nut.
And when he falls, he hurts his butt!

BIRTHDAY: November 13

Everyone in Blueberry's family eats fruit,
but not him. This nutty monkey prefers nuts!
It drives him bananas when someone insists
he should eat fruit salad. Yuck!

Bongo

PERSONALITY: Upbeat

FAVORITE FOOD OR DRINK:
Fried pineapple

LOVES: Laying down some
bodacious beats

HIS FRIENDS SAY: He's one
funky monkey.

SECRET TALENT: Beatboxing

PRIZED POSSESSION:
A set of golden bongos

PERSONAL POEM:
Swinging around the jungle trees
From vine to vine is such a breeze!

BIRTHDAY:
August 11

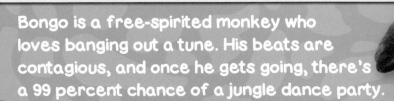

Bongo is a free-spirited monkey who
loves banging out a tune. His beats are
contagious, and once he gets going, there's
a 99 percent chance of a jungle dance party.

Boom Boom

R M
Mystic Mountains
Animal:
Panda

Everyone knows when Boom Boom is coming because her footsteps rumble like thunder. She's the lead drummer in the hit Beanie Boo band Bear Tracks, and she bangs the drums with her paws to keep the beat!

PERSONALITY: Loud and proud

FAVORITE FOOD OR DRINK: Crunchy bamboo

LOVES: Thunderstorms

ONE-HIT WONDER: "Boom Boom Ka-Pow"

PRIZED POSSESSION: Her bass drum

ENJOYS: Listening to echoes in the mountains

PERSONAL POEM:
I'm the coolest, loudest bear around.
I bang on the drum and make a big sound!

BIRTHDAY: June 4

All About Me!

Brutus

He may be a boxer, but Brutus is a total softie. He'll easily give you his heart and be your best buddy. The only thing he asks is that you don't make him do dog tricks—he can't stand them.

All About Me!

PERSONALITY: Softie

FAVORITE FOOD OR DRINK: Marshmallow spread

LOVES: Making new friends

DISLIKES: Dog tricks

SECRET HOBBY: Reading Shakespeare

HABIT: He wears his heart on his sleeve.

PERSONAL POEM:
You'll never know how much
   I care.
I'll give you big licks and follow
   you everywhere!

BIRTHDAY: September 2

Bubbly

PERSONALITY: Bright and bubbly

FAVORITE DRINK: Fizzy soda

LOVES: Bubble baths

FAVORITE SCENT: Sweet pea

MOTTO: Everyone needs time to relax.

BEST FRIEND: Zazzy the zebra

PERSONAL POEM:
My body is a lovely pink and green.
The best combo you've ever seen!

BIRTHDAY: June 9

One of Bubbly's favorite things to do is take bubble baths. She makes her own bubble-bath scents and always pours a few extra capfuls into the tub to make sure the bubbles pile up sky high.

Bubby

PERSONALITY: Happy

FAVORITE FOOD OR DRINK: Red-leaf lettuce

LOVES: Splashing in puddles

DISLIKES: Droughts

LITTLE KNOWN FACT: When it's about to rain, her ears wiggle!

FAVORITE MOVIE: *Singin' in the Rain*

PERSONAL POEM:
Spring will bloom the biggest flowers
When we get the April showers!

BIRTHDAY: April 24

Whenever Bubby sees a puddle, she splashes right in! Springtime showers are her favorite weather, and even though she owns a rainbow-colored umbrella, she rarely uses it. Getting wet is just too much fun!

23

RMC
Awesome Arctic Animal:
Lynx

Buckwheat

This shy little lynx tries his best to blend in, but those two pointy, furry ears make it hard sometimes! Buckwheat is a bit of a loner—he likes to stay close to his den. But his friends know how to coax him out for a game or two.

PERSONALITY: Shy

FAVORITE FOOD OR DRINK: Buckwheat waffles

LOVES: Making paw prints in the snow

DISLIKES: Sudden, loud noises

FAVORITE PASTIME: Watching the northern lights

NEVER LEAVES HOME WITHOUT: His baby blanket

PERSONAL POEM:
My ears are big with fluffy fur.
Hold me close and hear me purr.

BIRTHDAY: September 14

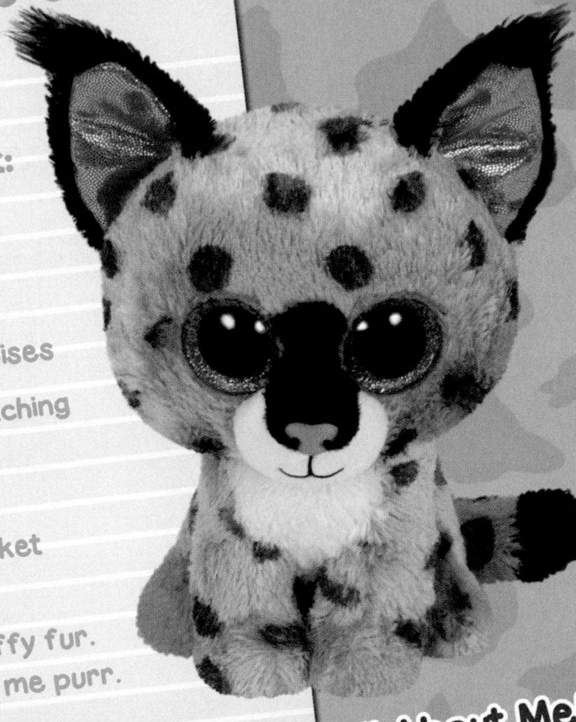

All About Me!

Bugsy

RMC
Friendly Field
Animal:
Ladybug

PERSONALITY: Lucky

FAVORITE FOOD OR DRINK: Ivy leaves

LOVES: Telling fortunes

DISLIKES: Ladders, broken mirrors, and black cats

BELIEVES: Good luck is always right around the corner.

RUMOR HAS IT: She can grant as many wishes as the spots on her back.

PERSONAL POEM:
I'm the luckiest bug you've
    ever seen.
My flying skills are
    also keen!

BIRTHDAY:
August 15

Bugsy is one lucky ladybug. She flies around the meadow telling her friends' fortunes and weaving them lucky charms out of wildflowers.

Butter

R
Fabulous Farm
Animal:
Cow

PERSONALITY: Hardworking

FAVORITE FOOD OR DRINK: Buttermilk

LOVES: Singing

FAVORITE SPOT:
The wide-open field where she can belt show tunes as loudly as she wants

DREAMS OF: Being onstage

ENJOYS: A *moo*-ving night of opera

PERSONAL POEM:
I don't talk, I only moo.
That's my way of saying "I love you."

BIRTHDAY: January 12

Butter has a special talent for singing opera all in "moos," and she likes to practice . . . *a lot*. Her rehearsals can last well into the night, keeping the whole farm awake!

Buzby

Whether he's flitting from flower to flower or bringing his friends fresh jars of honey, Buzby is one busy bee! He can fly superfast and loves having races with the butterflies in the field.

PERSONALITY: Energetic

FAVORITE FOOD OR DRINK: Honey water

LOVES: Buzzing along as fast as he can

FAVORITE FLOWER: Roses

SECRET WISH: To fly higher than the clouds!

DISLIKES: Rain really bugs him.

PERSONAL POEM:
I'm a very busy bee.
I fly so high it makes me dizzy.

BIRTHDAY: April 14

All About Me!

Cancun

R M EL C
Iridescent Islands
Animal:
Chihuahua

PERSONALITY: Spontaneous

FAVORITE FOOD OR DRINK: Tacos

LOVES: Snorkeling

ENJOYS: Fiestas

TEACHES: Windsurfing lessons

MOTTO: Party on, my friends.

PERSONAL POEM:
I'm a cute Chihuahua that loves
    the sun.
And my fabulous colors are lots
    of fun!

BIRTHDAY:
April 30

When Cancun is around, it's fiesta time!
This sun-loving doggy lives in the moment.
He's the go-to Beanie Boo for all sorts of
adventures and escapades.

Candy Cane

R
Marvelous
Metropolis
Animal:
Mouse

PERSONALITY: Cheerful

FAVORITE FOOD OR DRINK:
Peppermint candy canes

LOVES: Christmastime

FAVORITE ACCESSORY: A red-
and-white-striped scarf

SECRET TALENT: Singing carols
a cappella

LIVES IN: A Christmas
tree

PERSONAL POEM:
Candy canes are my favorite treat.
Holiday time just can't be beat!

BIRTHDAY:
December 4

Holiday spirit is in the air whenever Candy
Cane rolls into town. He's a tiny mouse with
a big sweet tooth, and he always makes
sure to bring an extra bag of treats for
his friends.

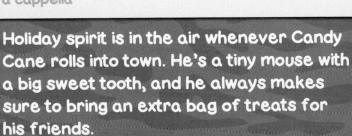

27

RC
Outrageous Ocean Animal: Turtle

Cara

Nothing makes Cara happier than watching the sun glint off the ocean's waves. She's a gentle soul who enjoys sharing the beauty of the sea with others.

PERSONALITY:
Compassionate

FAVORITE FOOD OR DRINK: Seaweed

LOVES: Sea, sun, and sand

DISLIKES: Litter on the beach

EARLIEST MEMORY: Crawling toward the ocean with all the other newborn turtles

TALENT: She's a natural teacher.

PERSONAL POEM:
I am a turtle, the Loggerhead kind.
My head is real big, and I live a long time.
The sea is my home, so I hope you understand.
When you play by my house, don't leave trash on the sand!

BIRTHDAY: March 1

All About Me!

Carrots has a twin sister who's brown!

Carrots

R M
Friendly Field
Animal:
Rabbit

PERSONALITY: Joyful

FAVORITE FOOD OR DRINK: Chocolate Easter eggs

LOVES: Baskets of treats

HABIT: Wiggling her nose

HOME: A grass-filled den in the carrot patch

KNOWN FOR: Surprising her friends

PERSONAL POEM:
My bunny ears really
   help me hear
When I deliver baskets
   One day a year!

BIRTHDAY:
February 1

Don't tell anyone, but Carrots is one of the Easter Bunny's main helpers! She hops around delivering baskets of goodies to children. Then she comes back to watch them hunt for eggs.

Casanova

R M C
Jazzy Jungle
Animal:
Monkey

PERSONALITY: Sweet-talking

FAVORITE FOOD OR DRINK: Chocolate-covered strawberries

LOVES: Falling in love

TALENT: Crafting homemade Valentines

HABIT: Writing love poems

FAVORITE HOLIDAY: Valentine's Day

PERSONAL POEM:
My temperature's high and
   my vision's a blur.
I have a bad case of jungle
Love for sure!

BIRTHDAY:
January 3

Casanova wears his heart on his sleeve—literally! He's a total charmer who gives candy hearts with sweet messages to all his friends.

Cashmere

Cashmere is a refined kitty who adores going to fashion shows to see the beautiful clothes. She dreams of becoming a fashion designer herself!

All About Me!

PERSONALITY: Refined

FAVORITE FOOD OR DRINK: Caviar

LOVES: High-tail fashion

FAVORITE DESIGNER:
Whisker de la Renta

TALENT: Sewing

DREAM VACATION:
A weeklong shopping spree
in Paris

PERSONAL POEM:
I'm a special cat with fancy fur.
And if I'm happy I sometimes purr!

BIRTHDAY: April 29

Charlotte

PERSONALITY: Electric

FAVORITE FOOD OR DRINK:
Energy drinks

LOVES: Bright colors

ENJOYS: Going and going and
going and going . . .

HER FRIENDS SAY: Charlotte is
always energized.

FAVORITE EXERCISE: Aerobics

PERSONAL POEM:
I always play with bells that ring
So I can jump and go ding-ding!

BIRTHDAY:
April 10

There's no mistaking Charlotte's pink-and-purple fur as she enters the room. Her bright colors are only second to her bright personality. When she's around, you can actually feel her energy!

Charming

RM
Jazzy Jungle
Animal:
Monkey

PERSONALITY: Adoring

FAVORITE FOOD OR DRINK:
Cherry limeade

LOVES: Giving roses to his friends

BEST FEATURE: His charming smile

HOPES: No one will break his heart

MENTOR: Casanova

PERSONAL POEM:
Happy Valentine's Day.
Here's my heart to lock away.

BIRTHDAY: February 26

Charming adores Valentine's Day so much, he actually colored his fur pink and red. He's a precious little fella who can't help giving his heart away to everyone he meets.

Cherry

R
Marvelous Metropolis
Animal: Dog

PERSONALITY: Regal

FAVORITE FOOD OR DRINK: Cherry-flavored ice pops

LOVES: Playing dress-up

FAVORITE SCHOOL ACTIVITY: Recess

PRIZED POSSESSION: Her princess diary

DRAWS PICTURES OF: Castles and dragons

PERSONAL POEM:
They all call me a pretty pink princess
Because I play with everyone at recess!

BIRTHDAY: June 2

Every night when Cherry goes to bed, dreams of tiaras and ball gowns dance in her head. Her cousin is a princess in a faraway country, so Cherry likes to think royalty runs in her family!

Chillz

R
Awesome Arctic
Animal: Penguin

PERSONALITY: Chill

FAVORITE FOOD: Frozen yogurt

LOVES: Ice baths

ALWAYS: Offers her friends a frosty beverage

PRIZED POSSESSION: An ice pinball machine

SECRET TALENT: Playing Ping-Pong

PERSONAL POEM:
My igloo looks so nice, I think.
I dyed the ice to make it pink!

BIRTHDAY: January 10

Chillz likes nothing more than chilling in her igloo. It's the perfect arctic hangout! She has her own frozen yogurt machine, and even a mini indoor ice pool!

Chloe

PERSONALITY: Lovable

FAVORITE FOOD OR DRINK: Animal crackers

LOVES: Giving licks

WANTS TO: Be a firefighter when she grows up

ENJOYS: Tickles!

FAVORITE GAME: Red Rover

PERSONAL POEM:
I'm the cutest dog you'll ever see.
Take me home and play with me!

BIRTHDAY: April 11

All About Me!

Chloe was born with a heart-shaped birthmark around her eye, and it fits her personality perfectly. She's an adorable Dalmatian with a huge heart, and she loves giving friendly licks.

RMLC
Fantastical Forest Animal: Dragon

Cinder

Cinder is a fiery-spirited dragon who can be a bit of a hotshot! She's very proud of her shimmering purple scales and enjoys showing off her flashy flying moves. But deep down, she just wants her friends to be proud of her.

PERSONALITY: Fiery

FAVORITE FOOD OR DRINK: Hot dogs

LOVES: Grilling

FANCIEST FLYING MOVE:
The Shimmering Spiral

KNOWN FOR: Hosting flame-grilled barbecues

SPECIAL DISH: Roasted Marshmallow Casserole

PERSONAL POEM:
Let's be friends and you will see
I'm happiest when you are with me!

BIRTHDAY: October 2

All About Me!

Clover

PERSONALITY: Lively

FAVORITE FOOD: Cabbage

LOVES: Frolicking

DISLIKES: Being too hot

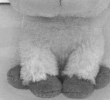

SECRET HOBBY: Looking for leprechauns in the meadow

PRIZED POSSESSION: Her lucky four-leaf clover

PERSONAL POEM:
Everyone thinks that I'm so cute.
And with my wool you
Can make a suit!

BIRTHDAY: February 2

Clover's favorite time of year is summertime, because that's when the lambs all get their wool sheared short. Clover would rather be cool and comfortable all year round!

Coconut

PERSONALITY: A little bit nutty

FAVORITE FOOD OR DRINK: Coconut cream pie

LOVES: Banging coconut shells together to make music

DISLIKES: Being called "short"

FAVORITE HANGOUT: A vine hammock draped between two coconut trees

MOTTO: Keep on swinging!

PERSONAL POEM:
Some say I'm a strange-looking monkey.
My legs are short and my body is chunky!

BIRTHDAY: July 27

Coconut may be a tiny monkey, but when he's around there's sure to be big fun! He's happy and zany and loves climbing trees to collect coconuts for his famous Coco-Loco parties!

Comet

Comet leaves a blazing trail of sparkles as he flies across the sky! His job is to pull Santa's sleigh with the other reindeer. To him, Christmas is the most wonderful time of the year!

PERSONALITY: Blazing

FAVORITE FOOD OR DRINK: Sugarplums

LOVES: Jingling sleigh bells

FAVORITE CHRISTMAS SONG: "Here Comes Santa Claus"

BEST FRIEND: Alpine

KNOWN FOR: Using his sparkle trail for skywriting

PERSONAL POEM:
I fly the sleigh very fast.
Holiday time is such a blast!

BIRTHDAY: December 3

All About Me!

Cookie

PERSONALITY: Hopeless romantic

FAVORITE FOOD OR DRINK:
Cheese pizza, doggy treats

LOVES: Valentine's Day

FAVORITE TOY: A stuffed bear
named Cupid

WISHES: She had a secret admirer

VALENTINE MESSAGE: When I
see you, I wag my tail. My love for
you will never fail!

PERSONAL POEM:
I very much like cheese pizza with
    meat.
But nothing compares to a doggy
    treat!

BIRTHDAY: August 2

Cookie positively hearts Valentine's Day. She can't get enough of it! The candy, the flowers, the *romance*. Her birthday is in August, but she prefers to celebrate her half birthday so she can celebrate closer to the day of love.

Cora

PERSONALITY: Antsy

FAVORITE FOOD: Sandwiches

LOVES: Traveling

PRIZED POSSESSION: Her
lucky suitcase

DISLIKES: Flight delays

MOTTO: Always plan ahead.

PERSONAL POEM:
I spend my days with family and
    friends
Enjoying the fun and sun on
    weekends!

BIRTHDAY: August 21

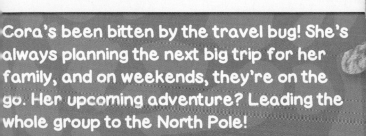

Cora's been bitten by the travel bug! She's always planning the next big trip for her family, and on weekends, they're on the go. Her upcoming adventure? Leading the whole group to the North Pole!

Corky

When Corky was born, she took her first steps in a field of sweet-smelling petunias. Ever since then, this little piggy has loved smelling lovely! She even wears a crown of flowers at springtime.

All About Me!

PERSONALITY: Squeaky clean

FAVORITE FOOD OR DRINK: Lemon squares

LOVES: Bath time

ALWAYS: Spritzes her pillow with rose water before bedtime

HOBBY: Making lavender mini pillows for her friends

MOTTO: Flower power!

PERSONAL POEM:
I'm the cleanest pig you ever
    did meet.
When I walk through mud, I wash
    my feet!

BIRTHDAY: April 21

Crawly

PERSONALITY: Creepy

FAVORITE FOOD: Candy corn

LOVES: Costumes

KNOWN FOR: Giving her friends a fright!

SECRET TALENT: Writing messages in webs

WISHES: More costumes came with eight legs

PERSONAL POEM:
Look at my frightful stare.
Cross me only if you dare!

BIRTHDAY:
September 21

Halloween only comes around once a year, and Crawly is determined to make the most of it. She tries on every costume before settling on the scariest look.

Cuddly Bear

RM
Fantastical Forest
Animal:
Bear

PERSONALITY: Careful

FAVORITE FOOD: Honeycomb

LOVES: Cuddles

LIVES IN: A cozy cottage with her parents

SECRET: Her heart has her name and address written on it, just in case she gets lost again.

NEVER LEAVES HOME WITHOUT: Her heart-shaped smartphone

PERSONAL POEM:
A bear with a heart, none cuter can be.
Please promise me that you'll never lose me!

BIRTHDAY:
May 7

When Cuddly was just a little cub, she accidently got lost in the forest. The unicorn Beanie Boos helped guide her home. Since then, this cuddly bear has been extra cautious.

Cutie Pie

Not many pandas live in the Marvelous Metropolis, but Cutie Pie isn't like most pandas. She runs the Cutie-Pie Pie Shop in the city center, and all her pies are shaped like hearts!

PERSONALITY: Warm

FAVORITE FOOD OR DRINK: Huckleberry Pie

LOVES: Baking

FAVORITE MEMORY: Helping her grandma roll pie crust as a cub

SIGNATURE PIE FLAVOR: Vanilla Apple Custard

CATCHPHRASE: Easy as pie!

PERSONAL POEM:
I'm cute and furry and we'll never part
If you just hold me close and warm
My cold heart.

BIRTHDAY: April 17

All About Me

Daisy

PERSONALITY: Simply pleasant

FAVORITE FOOD OR DRINK:
Dandelion tea

LOVES: Lazy mornings

APPRECIATES: An a-*moo*-sing joke

SECRET TALENT: She can play a mean banjo.

FAVORITE PASTIME: Spotting shapes in the clouds

PERSONAL POEM:
I love the country life, I really do.
Eating grass always makes me moo!

BIRTHDAY:
June 5

Daisy is a bright-eyed, fuzzy-tailed cow who is happiest with the simple things in life. She enjoys rolling in the grass, munching on daisies, and waking up at sunrise.

Dakota

PERSONALITY: Competitive

FAVORITE FOOD OR DRINK:
Apples

LOVES: Racing

DISLIKES: Coming in last

FAVORITE PLACE: The winner's circle

MOTTO: Time to run for the roses.

PERSONAL POEM:
The other horses can't keep pace.
I gallop to victory every race!

BIRTHDAY:
June 25

Every day is a day at the races when Dakota is around. This speedy horse will challenge anyone to a race, whether they're a horse, a bunny, or even a cheetah.

Dakota

R M
Marvelous
Metropolis
Animal:
Chihuahua

FAVORITE SCHOOL SUBJECT: Math

EARLIEST MEMORY: Counting to ten

MOTTO: You can count on me!

PERSONAL POEM:
Sit and stay I've learned to do.
And chew a bone instead of a shoe.

BIRTHDAY: June 13

PERSONALITY: Precise

FAVORITE FOOD: Pita chips

LOVES: Dotting i's and crossing t's

Dakota is very dedicated when it comes to following the rules. She's the treasurer of the Beanie Boos Student Council, and she always makes sure every dollar and cent is accounted for.

Dandelion

R
Marvelous
Metropolis
Animal:
Chihuahua

PERSONALITY: Helpful

FAVORITE FOOD OR DRINK: Cheesy enchiladas

LOVES: Sightseeing

FAVORITE SONG: "Follow the Yellow Brick Road"

ENJOYS: Visiting the local hot spots

FAVORITE TOY: A neon-orange traffic cone chew toy

PERSONAL POEM:
I like to bark when I hear noise,
Or play catch with all my toys.

BIRTHDAY: January 10

Dandelion's bright-yellow fur isn't just beautiful, it's really useful! She leads sightseeing tours through the Marvelous Metropolis. If any tourists happen to stray, they can spot her fur a mile away.

Darci

RMLC
Jazzy Jungle
Animal:
Giraffe

Darci is a high-class giraffe with a sophisticated upbringing. She attended a prestigious British academy before her family moved to the Jazzy Jungle. Now she helps teach the other jungle Beanie Boos proper manners, too!

PERSONALITY: Proper

FAVORITE FOOD OR DRINK: Peach sorbet

LOVES: Minding her manners

DISLIKES: Tall tales

GUILTY PLEASURE: Reading advice columns

WOULD NEVER: Slurp her soup

PERSONAL POEM:
Up high in the tree my neck reaches.
I grab a mouthful of fresh peaches!

BIRTHDAY: April 16

All About Me!

Daria

PERSONALITY: Artistic

FAVORITE DRINK: Herbal tea

LOVES: Painting

INSPIRATION: Mountain sunrises

ENJOYS: Meditating

PRIZED POSSESSION: A golden paintbrush

PERSONAL POEM:
One more reason for you to keep:
In 2015 it is the year of the sheep.

BIRTHDAY: February 18

The beauty of the Mystic Mountains has always inspired Daria. Then, one day, she started painting pictures of the landscapes. Now her home is filled with one-of-a-kind artwork!

Darla

PERSONALITY: Thoughtful

FAVORITE DRINK: Mint tea

LOVES: Riddles

PRIZED POSSESSION: An ancient puzzle box her grandfather gave her

DISLIKES: Taking the easy way out

FAVORITE PLACE:
Her soft cloud bed

PERSONAL POEM:
They say I'm bold, fun, and pink.
I love to do puzzles; they make me think.

BIRTHDAY:
May 25

Darla lives high in the Shimmering Sky on a fluffy pink cloud. She's an extremely smart dragon and spends her days creating puzzles and riddles to challenge her friends.

Darlin

R

Fabulous Farm
Animal:
Dog

PERSONALITY: Precious

FAVORITE FOOD OR DRINK:
Dog biscuits and gravy

LOVES: Country music

PRIZED POSSESSION:
Her lucky guitar pick

TALENT: Giving great hugs

FAVORITE MEMORY:
Her first concert

PERSONAL POEM:
I won't bark or chew your shoe.
I just want some hugs from you!

BIRTHDAY: February 10

All About Me!

Darlin has big dreams of being the lead singer in her own country music band. She even has a band name picked out: The Prairie Pups! Now she just needs to convince her friends to join, but with her puppy-dog eyes, who could refuse?

Darling

Paints, paints, paints—Darling can't get enough of brightly colored paints. She's a creative puppy with a flair for modern art, and she invented her own painting technique: Bubble Pop. She blows paint bubbles on a blank canvas and lets them pop, creating bright splatters of paint!

PERSONALITY: Artistic

FAVORITE FOOD OR DRINK: Cream soda

LOVES: Painting

INSPIRATION: Bubble gum and confetti

FAVORITE BIRTHDAY PARTY ACTIVITY: Paintball

SIGNS HER PAINTINGS: With a rainbow paw print

PERSONAL POEM:
Rainbow colors are what I prefer.
These colors look great all over my fur!

BIRTHDAY: February 2

All About Me

Dazzle

PERSONALITY: Dazzling

FAVORITE FOOD OR DRINK: Licorice

LOVES: Tap dancing

DANCE MOVE: The Rat-a-tat Tippity Tap

PRIZED POSSESSION: Her shiny black tap shoes

MOTTO: Razzle-dazzle 'em!

PERSONAL POEM:
Have you seen something so
   pretty
As a pink-and-black sparkling
   kitty?

BIRTHDAY: March 26

There's no business like show business, and Dazzle is determined to make it to the top. She's a pretty kitty who's quick on her paws, and she just knows she'll make it big with her special skill: tap dancing!

Dill

PERSONALITY: Hungry

FAVORITE FOOD OR DRINK: Pickles

LOVES: Backyard barbecues

DISLIKES: Cucumbers

MOST EMBARRASSING MOMENT: The time he got his paw stuck in the pickle jar

FAVORITE PASTIME: Rolling in the grass

PERSONAL POEM:
I'm not a pickle, but I'm very green.
If I hide in the grass, I'll never be
   seen.

BIRTHDAY: June 20

Whenever Dill goes to a barbecue, he skips the grill and heads straight for the pickles! He just can't help himself—when he has a hankering, nothing else will do.

Diva

Diva can spend hours in front of the mirror primping, but beneath her glitz and glamour, she has a big heart. She's always ready to lend her friends a helping paw.

PERSONALITY: Glamorous

FAVORITE FOOD OR DRINK: Sunflower seeds

LOVES: Getting dolled up

NEVER LEAVES HOME WITHOUT: A jeweled comb

FAVORITE SPOT: Her pink dressing room

ENJOYS: Watching old Hollywood movies

PERSONAL POEM: My pink ears are pretty for sure. They go so well with my white fur!

BIRTHDAY: October 13

All About Me

Dotty

PERSONALITY: Vivacious

FAVORITE FOOD OR DRINK:
Banana chocolate-chip pancakes

LOVES: Being in the spotlight

DISLIKES: Blending in

FAVORITE HOBBY: Dancing

MOTTO: Be bold!

PERSONAL POEM:
If you stare at my bold-colored
　　spots,
They might start to look like big
　　crazy dots!

BIRTHDAY: June 16

Dotty's colorful spots make her one of a kind.
While most leopards in the Mystic Mountains
like to blend in, Dotty loves standing out! She's
known for her signature dance move, the
Dizzy Dot.

Dougie

R
Fabulous Farm
Animal:
Dog

PERSONALITY: Down and dirty

FAVORITE FOOD OR DRINK:
Mud pies

LOVES: Digging

DISLIKES: Bath time

ENJOYS: Rainstorms—they make
great puddles!

FAVORITE GAME: Mud wrestling

PERSONAL POEM:
I shake my toy; it makes a sound,
Then I'll bury it in the ground!

BIRTHDAY: December 20

Dougie isn't afraid to get his paws dirty.
He romps around the Fabulous Farm,
chasing sticks, burying toys, and digging
in the dirt. If he spots a puddle, he'll dive
right in—the muddier the better!

49

Dreamer

PERSONALITY: Dreamy

FAVORITE FOOD OR DRINK: Iced chamomile tea

LOVES: Hearing about her friends' best dreams

HOBBY: Weaving dream catchers

PRIZED POSSESSION: Her dream journal

CATCHPHRASE: Sweet dreams!

PERSONAL POEM:
I am happy that you're my best
    friend.
And I know our friendship will
    never, never end!

BIRTHDAY:
November 8

It may be bright and sunny in the jungle, but that won't stop Dreamer from dreaming the day away. You can usually find her curled up on a high jungle branch, snoozing soundly.

Duchess

PERSONALITY: Sassy

FAVORITE FOOD OR DRINK: Chips and salsa

LOVES: Mariachi bands

LIKES THINGS: Hot and spicy!

DISLIKES: Formal events

PARENTS: The Duke and Duchess of *Canine*-bridge

PERSONAL POEM:
I'm a Chihuahua with lots of flair.
I have sparkly eyes and rainbow
    hair!

BIRTHDAY: January 12

Duchess's family is technically royalty, but she isn't really the regal type. She prefers salsa dancing to ballroom dancing, and intends to rock royalty her own way!

Duke

R M
Marvelous
Metropolis
Animal:
Dog

Duke is a *bone*-a-fide champ when it comes to athletic competitions. Whether he's running in a race, dog-paddling in the pool, or perfecting his Downward Dog yoga position, you can be sure he's giving it 100 percent.

All About Me!

PERSONALITY: Pumped up

FAVORITE FOOD OR DRINK: T-bone steaks

LOVES: Exercise

MOTTO: You can do it!

ENJOYS: Teaching his friends new tricks

PERSONAL GOAL: To earn a black belt in karate

PERSONAL POEM:
Running makes me a happy dog.
So take me with you when you jog!

BIRTHDAY: May 20

Elfie

RL
Jazzy Jungle
Animal:
Elephant

PERSONALITY: Energized

FAVORITE FOOD OR DRINK:
Peanut-butter ice cream

LOVES: Playing in the sun

ALWAYS: Wears sunscreen

FAVORITE VACATION: A trip to
the peanut plantation

MOTTO: Sharing is caring.

PERSONAL POEM:
I love to eat peanuts in the sun
And share with my friends one
  by one.

BIRTHDAY:
October 18

Elfie is nuts about peanuts! They're her
favorite snack. She likes to stack bags
of peanuts around the jungle to make
little forts that she can munch from.

Ellie

RML
Jazzy Jungle
Animal:
Elephant

PERSONALITY: Loud

FAVORITE FOOD OR DRINK:
Squash

LOVES: A good beat

DISLIKES: When it's too quiet

KNOWN FOR: Being a team player

MOTTO: Live out loud!

PERSONAL POEM:
When I stomp across the ground
It always makes a great big sound!

BIRTHDAY: August 27

Ellie is always moving and grooving. She's on her
neighborhood's stomp team, where they clap and stomp their
feet to the rhythm of a drumbeat. Sometimes, Ellie gets a
special solo where she stomps all by herself!

Fairbanks

PERSONALITY: Festive

FAVORITE FOOD OR DRINK:
Sugar cookies

LOVES: His cozy sleigh bed

HIS FRIENDS SAY: Fairbanks
brings good food and good cheer!

SILLY STORY: The time he slipped
on the ice and dropped a whole
batch of cookies!

SECRET: Santa's elves modeled a toy
after him for Christmastime.

PERSONAL POEM:
My good friend Santa says the time is near.
So Happy Holidays and Happy New Year!

BIRTHDAY: December 1

All About Me!

Fairbanks says he can smell the holiday
season, but it's probably just because that's
when he starts to bake his famous snowflake
sugar cookies. He gives them to his friends as
gifts.

Fantasia

All About Me!

PERSONALITY: Optimistic

FAVORITE FOOD OR DRINK:
Cotton candy

LOVES: Wishing stars

DISLIKES: Frowns

ENJOYS: Galloping through
the trees

MOTTO: Dream big!

PERSONAL POEM:
Come close . . . I have a secret for you.
I wish your dreams and wishes come true.

BIRTHDAY: May 8

Fantasia lives deep in the Fantastical Forest
with her unicorn pals. She believes that if you
can dream it, you can achieve it! When her
friends get upset, Fantasia can always cheer
them up with a smile, a song, or some great
advice.

Feathers

R
Fabulous Farm
Animal:
Turkey

PERSONALITY: Energetic

FAVORITE FOOD OR DRINK: Corn bread

LOVES: Running in circles

DISLIKES: Nap time

EARLIEST MEMORY: Getting lost in a haystack!

ENJOYS: Corn mazes

PERSONAL POEM:
My feathers are so big and bright.
They keep me warm all day
and night!

BIRTHDAY: May 9

Feathers is a little ball of energy, running around the farm and showing off his brilliant red and brown colors. He plays so much during the day that he falls right asleep at night, but he's up again with the rooster's crow, ready to play some more.

Fetch

R M C
Marvelous
Metropolis
Animal:
Dog

PERSONALITY: Precise

FAVORITE FOOD OR DRINK: Spaghetti and tomato sauce

LOVES: Playing in the yard

PRIZED POSSESSION: His Frisbees

ENJOYS: Trips to the Friendly Field

CATCHPHRASE: Catch me if you can!

PERSONAL POEM:
To run and jump is always fun.
At catching Frisbees, I'm #1!

BIRTHDAY:
August 23

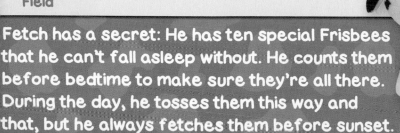

Fetch has a secret: He has ten special Frisbees that he can't fall asleep without. He counts them before bedtime to make sure they're all there. During the day, he tosses them this way and that, but he always fetches them before sunset.

Fiona

RMLC
Friendly Field
Animal:
Cat

PERSONALITY: Jumpy

FAVORITE FOOD OR DRINK: Banana bread

LOVES: Catnip

DISLIKES: Fences

ENJOYS: The thrill of the chase

FAVORITE STORYBOOK: *Three Little Kittens*

PERSONAL POEM:
I chased a mouse down from the
  willow.
Then he crawled under my pillow!

BIRTHDAY: August 31

Fiona is always alert and ready to pounce on everything in sight—from balls and toys to mice. To her, it's just a game, but the mice aren't very happy about it!

Firecracker

R
Marvelous
Metropolis
Animal:
Cat

PERSONALITY: Proud

FAVORITE FOOD OR DRINK: Jalapeño poppers

LOVES: Celebrations

ALWAYS: Goes out with a bang

SIGNATURE FIREWORK: The Red, White, and Blue Spiral Sparkler

FAVORITE HOLIDAY: Independence Day

PERSONAL POEM:
I like firecrackers that
  are red and blue.
And I want to celebrate
  the day with you!

BIRTHDAY: July 1

Every Fourth of July, Firecracker leads the Marvelous Metropolis's fireworks display. He searches for the best and brightest firecrackers, and even gets some magical ones from the unicorns. At sunset, everyone gathers to watch the show. It's really something!

Flippy

PERSONALITY: Lively

FAVORITE FOOD OR DRINK:
Seaweed chips

LOVES: Acrobatics

DISLIKES: Small
spaces

CAPTAIN OF:
The School of Fish
Gymnastics Team

MOTTO: Just dive in!

PERSONAL POEM:
I have big fins and I'm really cool.
They really sparkle when I'm in the pool!

BIRTHDAY: January 3

All About Me!

Flippy is the most acrobatic fish you'll ever meet. She's always flipping in and out of the water! Her favorite move is her Fliptastic Flip, where she jumps high and twirls three times before splashing back into the waves.

Flips

PERSONALITY: Determined

FAVORITE FOOD OR DRINK:
Mangoes

LOVES: Ballet

WOULD NEVER: Settle for less
than her very best

FAVORITE BALLET: Swan Lake

PRIZED POSSESSION: Her
collection of tutus

PERSONAL POEM:
I'm the smartest in the sea,
So learning tricks comes
   naturally!

BIRTHDAY: March 25

Ever since Flips was a little dolphin, it's been her dream to be
an underwater ballerina. She choreographs her own dance
routines and practices every day, and her friends say she's
quite talented. They know she'll make her dream come true!

Flora

PERSONALITY: Sweet

FAVORITE FOOD OR DRINK:
Lavender macarons

LOVES: Fields of lovely smelling
flowers

FAVORITE HANGOUT:
A bed of cushy moss in the
Fantastical Forest

DISLIKES: Mud

FAVORITE BIRTHDAY GIFT:
A dress Pixy the unicorn
made for her entirely out of roses!

PERSONAL POEM:
I am black and white and pink,
And every now and then I stink.

BIRTHDAY:
April 6

Flora is an incredibly sweet skunk with
an unfortunately unsweet smell. But she
goes out of her way to make her friends
feel special, and they love her for it.

Fluffy

R
Jazzy Jungle
Animal:
Lion

You would think that roaring sounds scary, but somehow, Fluffy makes it sound cute. She's an adorable lion who blushes at the drop of a hat. In fact, she blushes so much, it makes her fur look pink!

All About Me!

PERSONALITY: Adorable

FAVORITE FOOD OR DRINK: Chocolate lava cake

LOVES: Brushing her fur

KNOWN FOR: Giving out candygrams on Valentine's Day

FAVORITE TOY: A little stuffed giraffe named Suzy

SECRET: She sometimes dreams she's the queen of the jungle!

PERSONAL POEM:

My hair always gets stuck in a
brush.
Just sing me a song to make
me blush!

BIRTHDAY: February 23

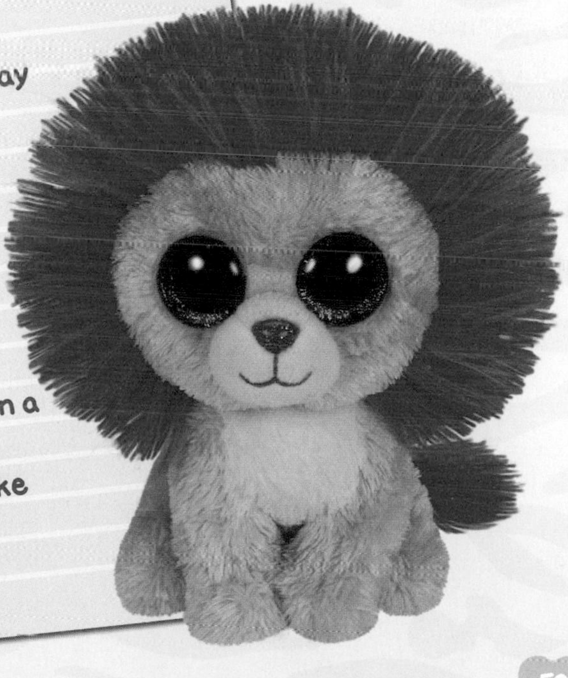

Franky

LOVES: Playing Hide-and-Boo Seek among the trees in the Fantastical Forest

BEST FRIEND: Owen the owl

PERSONAL POEM:
Let's play hide and then go seek,
But just make sure you never peek.

PERSONALITY: Playful

FAVORITE FOOD OR DRINK: Honey graham crackers

BIRTHDAY: October 17

In the Fantastical Forest, Franky is famous for her fun-loving personality. She loves playing games with the other animals, especially Hide-and-Boo Seek. But look out if you're one of the hiders—Franky's got a reputation for being the fastest seeker around!

Freeze

R M
Awesome Arctic
Animal:
Penguin

PERSONALITY: Wobbly

FAVORITE DRINK: Eggnog

LOVES: Building snow forts

KNOWN FOR: Sliding across the frozen pond on his belly

FAVORITE GAME: Snowball fights

FAVORITE TREAT: Warm cocoa

PERSONAL POEM:
My little red hat keeps me snuggly
    and warm.
I can play all day long in a really
    bad storm.

BIRTHDAY: November 17

Freeze never leaves his igloo without his woolly red hat. His grandmother knit it for him as a special Christmas gift. That's why it's just the right size for Freeze's little penguin head!

Frights

PERSONALITY: Scaredy-cat

FAVORITE FOOD OR DRINK: Vanilla custard

LOVES: Warm, cozy fires

DISLIKES: Creepy shadows

KNOWN FOR: Having one orange eye and one green eye

SPOOKIEST DREAM: That he was being carried away by a bat

PERSONAL POEM:
They tell me I'm a scary cat
Because I can hide in a witch's hat!

BIRTHDAY: October 19

Frights doesn't want to be a scaredy-cat, but the poor little guy is afraid of his own shadow. When Frights is startled, he can jump ten feet in the air. Luckily, he always lands on his feet.

Gabby

R
Fabulous Farm
Animal:
Goat

PERSONALITY: Playful

FAVORITE FOOD OR DRINK: Mozzarella sticks

LOVES: Playing with her friends

DISLIKES: Bedtime

FAVORITE GAME: Hide-and-goat seek

PRIZED POSSESSION: Her Barnyard Games trophy

PERSONAL POEM:
Let me be your very best friend.
Then our playtime will never end.

BIRTHDAY: June 2

Gabby is one of the most playful Beanie Boos on the farm. She loves staying up late to play games in the dark, and when her mom calls her home, she always asks for a few more minutes.

Gatsby

PERSONALITY: Imaginative

FAVORITE FOOD: Sea biscuits

LOVES: Pirates

DREAMS OF: Going on grand adventures!

PRIZED POSSESSION: An old compass his granddad dog gave him

FAVORITE BOOK: *The Legend of Blackbeard*

PERSONAL POEM:
I like it when you read to me
About pirates and the deep
    blue sea!

BIRTHDAY:
July 24

If ever there was a sea-loving sea dog, it's Gatsby. He's sailed around the world in search of fortune and brought back tales of pirates at sea . . . at least, that's what he likes to pretend.

George

RMC

Jazzy Jungle
Animal:
Gorilla

PERSONALITY: Chatterbox

FAVORITE FOOD OR DRINK:
Green tea cupcakes

LOVES: Having a good chat 'n' chew

DISLIKES: Secrets

FAVORITE GOSSIP MAGAZINE:
The Jungle Rumble

MOTTO: You can tell me anything!

PERSONAL POEM:
I get excited when my friends
    visit me.
We talk and eat fruit,
    while we sip on our tea.

BIRTHDAY:
October 18

George knows everything that's going on in the jungle, and he has a habit of sharing everyone's news with everyone else. He just can't help spilling the beans!

Georgia

All About Me!

PERSONALITY: Diligent

FAVORITE FOOD OR DRINK: Donuts

LOVES: Coming to the rescue

PROUD OF: The time she rescued a baby kitten from being stuck up a tree

ENJOYS: Sliding down the fire pole

MOTTO: Stop, drop, and roll.

PERSONAL POEM:
The firehouse is where I stay.
The siren sounds, no time for play!

BIRTHDAY: March 14

Whenever the fire alarm sounds, Georgia is at the ready! She rides on the Marvelous Metropolis fire truck and helps the firefighters wherever there's trouble. She knows that when it comes to fire safety, there's no playing around!

Ghosty

RMC
Marvelous
Metropolis
Animal:
Ghost

PERSONALITY: Spooky

FAVORITE FOOD OR DRINK:
Ghost pops

LOVES: Quiet evenings

DISLIKES: Creaky floors

LIVES IN: A haunted house

SECRET HOBBY: Eavesdropping

PERSONAL POEM:
I float around a haunted home;
From room to room is where
    I roam!

BIRTHDAY:
October 29

Some ghosts boo, other ghosts rattle and bang chains. But not Ghosty. He's completely quiet as he floats around his old haunted house. His friends say he's a good listener.

Ghoulie

RM
Marvelous
Metropolis
Animal:
Ghost

PERSONALITY: Frightening

FAVORITE FOOD OR DRINK:
Orange witches' brew

LOVES: Scaring unsuspecting trick-or-treaters

MOTTO: It's cool to be a ghoul.

HOBBY: Boo-beatboxing

FAVORITE TIME:
Midnight

PERSONAL POEM:
I am the scariest ghost in town.
Don't ever mistake me for a clown!

BIRTHDAY: October 8

Ghoulie is as loud as ghosts come! He'll frighten his friends with a loud "BOO!" when they least expect it. He even comes up with his own Boo-beatboxing raps to perform at Halloween.

Gilbert

RMC
Sunny Savannah
Animal:
Giraffe

With his tall legs and bright-purple spots, Gilbert was born to stick out. He's a terrific athlete and can play almost any sport, but his favorite is volleyball. He loves leading his team to victory!

All About Me!

PERSONALITY: Encouraging

FAVORITE FOOD OR DRINK: Peanut butter

LOVES: Playing sports

DISLIKES: Unfair referees

SPECIAL VOLLEYBALL SHOT: The Gilbert Spike

MOTTO: You miss all the shots you don't take.

PERSONAL POEM:
I like to lick peanut butter
   off a spoon.
But my mouth gets real sticky,
   so I can't sing a tune.

BIRTHDAY: August 23

R M
Iridescent Islands
Animal:
Flamingo

Gilda

All About Me!

PERSONALITY: Silly

FAVORITE FOOD OR DRINK: Raspberry slushies

LOVES: Making her friends laugh

FAVORITE MOVIE: A good comedy

LITTLE KNOWN FACT: She has seven brothers and sisters!

PRIZED POSSESSION:
The first-place ribbon she won in *Last Comedian Standing (On One Leg)*

PERSONAL POEM:
I like to tell jokes and act real silly.
I am funnier than my brother Billy!

BIRTHDAY: February 26

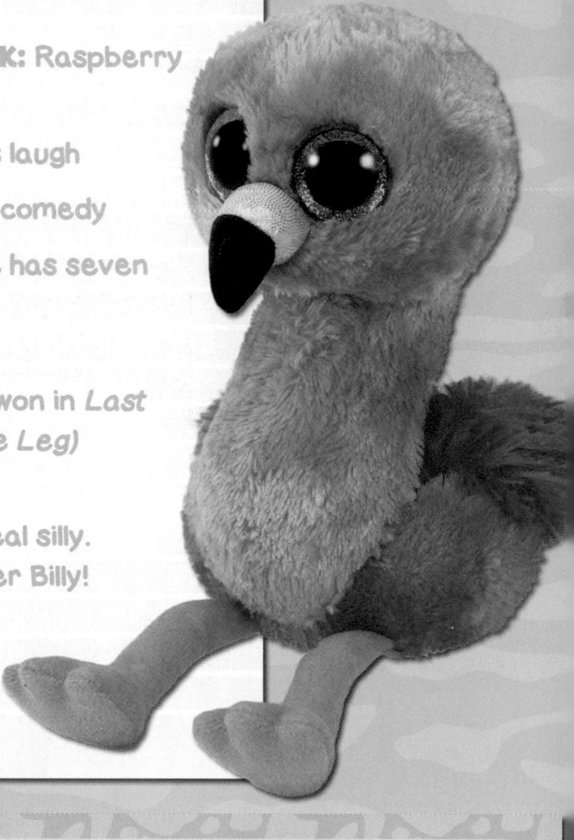

Gilda is the silliest flamingo of her flock! She's quick with a joke and even quicker with a punch line. Her special trick is doing stand-up comedy while standing on one foot.

Glamour

RMLELC
Jazzy Jungle
Animal:
Leopard

PERSONALITY: Confident

FAVORITE FOOD: Hazelnuts

LOVES: Fashion shows

FAVORITE LOOK: Leopard print, of course

SECRET HOBBY: Watching soap operas

KNOWN FOR: Giving great life advice

PERSONAL POEM:
What kinda leopard is purple and
  pink?
The prettiest one, I surely think!

BIRTHDAY:
January 20

With her sparkling eyes and dazzling fur, Glamour's got it going *on*. This fearless feline treats every jungle path like a runway. Her confidence is contagious.

Glider

RMLC
Awesome Arctic
Animal:
Penguin

PERSONALITY: Inventive

FAVORITE FOOD OR DRINK: Frozen bananas

LOVES: Winter sports

DREAM: To join the Boolympics Ice Luge Team

BOOLYMPIC HERO: Brian Boo-tano

MOTTO: Go for gold!

PERSONAL POEM:
I glide on the ice and rest in the
  sun.
Then I make a big splash, and
  that's a lot of fun!

BIRTHDAY:
August 4

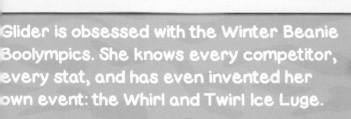

Glider is obsessed with the Winter Beanie Boolympics. She knows every competitor, every stat, and has even invented her own event: the Whirl and Twirl Ice Luge.

Gobbler

PERSONALITY: Serious

FAVORITE FOOD OR DRINK: Green beans

LOVES: A frank conversation

DISLIKES: Thanksgiving. He gets a little anxious on the big day.

LOOKS AFTER: His younger brother

WISHES: Christmas would come early.

PERSONAL POEM:
Thanksgiving is the only day
That makes me nervous, I have to say!

BIRTHDAY: November 17

Gobbler and his younger brother, Gobbles, live on the Fabulous Farm. He's a serious bird and likes to talk turkey. But he gobbles so much, his conversations can sound like gobbledygook!

Gobbles

PERSONALITY: Playful

FAVORITE FOOD OR DRINK: Berry cobbler

LOVES: Autumn

DISLIKES: Being a cold turkey

ALWAYS: Listens to his older brother

FAVORITE GAME: Jumping in leaves

PERSONAL POEM:
When I give a gobble or two,
I'm simply saying "Hello" to you!

BIRTHDAY: November 28

Gobbles is Gobbler's playful younger brother. He runs around like a wild turkey! His favorite time of year is autumn. He loves to make big piles of leaves and leap into them.

Goldie

R
Fabulous Farm
Animal:
Chick

All the Beanie Boos love to coo over Goldie—
she's just the sweetest little chick on the farm.
She only hatched from her egg a short while
ago, and the world is a big, brand-new place to
her!

All About Me!

PERSONALITY: Sweet and a little shy

FAVORITE FOOD OR DRINK: Worms

LOVES: Her cozy nest

STAYS CLOSE TO:
Her mama

EARLIEST MEMORY:
Hatching just last week!

CATCHPHRASE: Cheep,
cheep, cheep!

PERSONAL POEM:
I like to hop and cannot fly.
I'm also just
A little shy!

BIRTHDAY:
March 29

Grapes

Grapes spends his days swinging from vine to vine in the Jazzy Jungle looking for fresh fruit to munch on. He's always willing to share his fruit stash with his friends . . . except for his bananas. Those he keeps all to himself!

PERSONALITY: Peppy

FAVORITE FOOD OR DRINK: Bananas

LOVES: The smell of fresh berries

DISLIKES: Stale fruitcake

SECRET TALENT: Juggling fruit

KNOWN FOR: Hanging upside down from the jungle vines

PERSONAL POEM:
I swing in the trees. I leap all around.
If you give me bananas, I'll jump on the ground!

BIRTHDAY: April 1

All About Me!

Grimm

PERSONALITY: Grim

FAVORITE FOOD OR DRINK: Nothing. He doesn't get hungry much.

LOVES: Hourglasses

TENDS TO: Make people nervous

KNOWN FOR: Showing up when least expected

MOTTO: Don't be afraid.

PERSONAL POEM:
I like to tell real spooky stories.
But none of them will be real gory!

BIRTHDAY: July 14

Grimm doesn't have many friends. Maybe it's his ominous personality, or the fact that he's just downright . . . spooky. Wherever he goes, a dark cloud follows.

Gypsy

PERSONALITY: Nomadic

FAVORITE FOOD OR DRINK: Fresh-baked bread

LOVES: Traveling

TENDS TO: Stick out wherever she goes

PRIZED POSSESSION: A pink crystal ball

TALENT: Telling fascinating stories

PERSONAL POEM:
The spots on my fur look great I think.
But the best part is I'm a FABULOUS pink!

BIRTHDAY: April 28

Gypsy used to live in the Jazzy Jungle, but it was too hot for her taste. Then she tried the Mystic Mountains, but the snow wasn't her style. She's been happy in the Friendly Field, but her mice neighbors are a little less so.

Halo

PERSONALITY: Angelic

FAVORITE FOOD OR DRINK: Angel food cake

LOVES: Keeping watch

FAVORITE COLOR: Pearly white

FAVORITE SONG: "Pennies from Heaven"

MOTTO: Miracles happen every day.

PERSONAL POEM:
When you sleep I'm always here.
Don't be afraid, I am near.
Watching over you with lots of love:
Your guardian angel from up above!

BIRTHDAY: June 19

Every Beanie Boo needs a guardian angel like Halo. She watches over her friends from high up on her fluffy white cloud. As long as she's around, Beanie Boos know they're safe.

Harmonie

LOVES: Breaking into song

KNOWN FOR: Catching rays by Rainbow Bridge

MOTTO: Shut up and SING!

PERSONAL POEM:
I sing because it's a lot of fun,
But only when I sit in the sun.

BIRTHDAY: September 7

PERSONALITY: Sunny

FAVORITE FOOD OR DRINK: Cupcakes with rainbow sprinkles

Most unicorns are known for being a bit shy, but not Harmonie. She loves to sing, especially in front of an audience. On sunny days, you can find her by Rainbow Bridge, catching rays and practicing her favorite tunes.

Harriet

PERSONALITY: Team player

FAVORITE FOOD OR DRINK: Carrots

LOVES: Galloping

DISLIKES: Complaining

KNOWN FOR: Cheering on her friends

MOTTO: We can do it!

PERSONAL POEM:
I'm very important and my name is
    Harriet,
Because my special job is to lead
    the chariot!

BIRTHDAY:
December 20

Harriet is a hardworking horse who takes her job seriously. It's her responsibility to lead the chariot during the Beanie Boos' Fall Festival! The fair only happens once a year, and Harriet knows it's her time to shine.

Haunt

PERSONALITY: Mischievous

FAVORITE FOOD OR DRINK: Chocolate peanut-butter cups

LOVES: Pulling pranks

FAVORITE HAUNT: The Night Owl Cafe

BEST PRANK: When he scared Ghoulie the ghost by pretending to be a flying mummy!

FAVORITE DANCE: The Monster Mash

PERSONAL POEM:
My body is covered in
    orange and black
From head to toe and
    front and back!

BIRTHDAY:
October 22

Haunt is his name, and mischief is his game. This tricky owl is more about tricks than treats on Halloween night. He'll fly around pretending to be a monster that goes bump in the night. Talk about a hoot!

Holly

Bright and early in the morning, Holly shuffles through the forest, sniffing for tasty mushrooms. The sunrise reflects off her fur, casting beautiful colors throughout the woods. Her friends say it's like being woken up by a rainbow every morning!

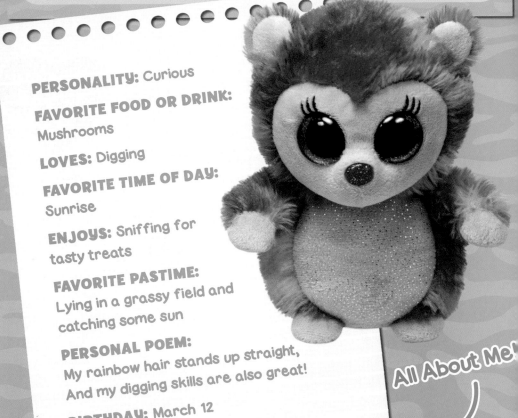

PERSONALITY: Curious

FAVORITE FOOD OR DRINK: Mushrooms

LOVES: Digging

FAVORITE TIME OF DAY: Sunrise

ENJOYS: Sniffing for tasty treats

FAVORITE PASTIME: Lying in a grassy field and catching some sun

PERSONAL POEM:
My rainbow hair stands up straight,
And my digging skills are also great!

BIRTHDAY: March 12

All About Me!

74

Honey

RMC Fantastical Forest Animal: Bear

DISLIKES: The dentist

HER FRIENDS SAY: She has a sweet personality because she eats so many sweets!

HOSTS: Honey fondue parties

PERSONAL POEM:
I love to eat all kinds of treats. Sometimes my dinner is only sweets!

BIRTHDAY: December 14

PERSONALITY: Friendly

FAVORITE FOOD OR DRINK: Pecan-honey caramels

LOVES: Sugary sweets

Honey knows she shouldn't eat so many sweets, but she can't help herself. Chocolates? Yes, please! Gummies? More like yummies! She'll gobble up every treat and still have room for dessert.

Honey Bun

RM Marvelous Metropolis Animal: Dog

PERSONALITY: Adorable

FAVORITE FOOD: Honey buns

LOVES: Making friends (with everyone)

KNOWN FOR: Following her heart

PRIZED POSSESSION: Her heart-shaped friendship locket

CATCHPHRASE: I'll stick to you like honey on a bun.

PERSONAL POEM:
I give you my heart, my sweet
    honey bun.
Together we're great and have
    lots of fun.

BIRTHDAY: February 5

Honey Bun loves making friends. Sometimes she runs up to complete strangers and licks them! But with her big, bright eyes and adorable little bark, who could resist her?

Hopson

RM
Friendly Field
Animal:
Rabbit

PERSONALITY: Hip

FAVORITE FOOD OR DRINK:
Carrot smoothies

LOVES: Hip-hop dancing

SIGNATURE DANCE MOVE: The
Jump Thump

PRIZED POSSESSION: Her lucky
sneakers

**ALWAYS HAS HER RADIO TUNED
TO:** 97.6—Boo Bunny Beatz

PERSONAL POEM:
From here to there I hop around.
Visiting friends all over town!

BIRTHDAY:
March 31

Rumor has it Hopson has been hippity-hopping nonstop since the day she was born. Hopson is always on the go. She even teaches her own hip-hop class on weekends.

Ice Cube

RML
Awesome Arctic
Animal:
Penguin

PERSONALITY: Rough and tumble

FAVORITE FOOD: Snow cones

LOVES: Playing ice hockey

SPECIAL MOVE: The
Slip-n-Slide Slapshot

KNOWN FOR: Winging it on the
rink

ENJOYS: Chilling to some
cool tunes

PERSONAL POEM:
I shuffle through the Arctic snow,
Then slip on ice and away I go!

BIRTHDAY: February 11

Ice Cube may be tiny, but don't let that fool you into thinking he's weak. This dude is tough as walrus tusks, especially when it comes to ice hockey! He slips past opponents and scores goals in a flash!

Iceberg

Iceberg lives on a floating piece of ice drifting around the Awesome Arctic. He enjoys the free lifestyle, gliding from place to place and visiting friends.

PERSONALITY:
Free-spirited

FAVORITE FOOD OR DRINK: Frozen fish

LOVES: Going where the wind takes him

DISLIKES: Cruise ships. They get in his way.

HOBBY: Ice fishing

BEST FEATURE: His icy-blue eyes

PERSONAL POEM:
I like to eat my favorite dish:
A snow cone and a couple of fish!

BIRTHDAY: July 2

All About Me!

Icicles

PERSONALITY: Diligent

FAVORITE FOOD OR DRINK: Warmed ginger beer

LOVES: Holiday spirit

FAVORITE CHRISTMAS SIGHT: Lights twinkling like icicles from roof eaves

PRIZED POSSESSION: A crocheted icicle ornament from Mrs. Claus

FAVORITE SONG: "Owl Be Home For Christmas"

PERSONAL POEM:
Winter is a chilly flight for me.
To warm up I hide in
the trunk of a
tree.

BIRTHDAY: December 12

Icicles is one of Santa's dedicated messenger owls. He delivers letters to the reindeer and elves in the Awesome Arctic. It can be cold, but his fleecy hat keeps him warm.

Icy

PERSONALITY: CUTE

FAVORITE FOOD: Fish sticks

LOVES: Giving Eskimo kisses

HOME: A cozy little den in the snow

FAVORITE PASTIME: Watching for shooting stars

DREAMS OF: Lots and lots of fish!

PERSONAL POEM:
I swim in the ocean
and lay on the ice.
My pretty white coat, they say,
is quite nice.
To put on my blubber, I eat lots
of fish.
I catch them quickly when they
start to swish!

BIRTHDAY: February 27

Icy is the most adorable seal pup EVER! She's plump and fluffy like a marshmallow, and she makes the sweetest chattering noise as she burrows into the snow. Icy can't help it—cute just looks good on her!

Igloo

PERSONALITY: Welcoming

FAVORITE FOOD OR DRINK:
Peppermint bark

LOVES: Hosting guests

KNOWN FOR: Preparing
the best breakfast
in the North Pole

VACATIONS: On an
iceberg in the North Sea

ENJOYS: Decorating the
igloos for Christmastime

PERSONAL POEM:
I love the snowy Arctic air
And chillin' on icebergs without a care!

BIRTHDAY: January 4

All About Me!

Igloo runs one of the only bed-and-breakfasts
north of the Arctic Circle. Every room looks like
a mini igloo, and guests are treated to frosty
sparkling cider and peppermint patties. Igloo's
B&B may be chilly, but you're always guaranteed
a warm welcome!

Igor

RM
Mystic Mountains
Animal:
Bat

PERSONALITY: Shady

FAVORITE FOOD OR DRINK:
Ghoul-ash

LOVES: Lightning storms

SLEEPS IN: The attic

FAVORITE FILMS: Monster movies

CATCHPHRASE: Yes, Master.

PERSONAL POEM:
I like to sleep hanging upside down.
And then I fly all over town!

BIRTHDAY:
September 7

Igor lives in a spooky old house located on top of a mountain. Beanie Boos swear they hear strange cackles echoing from inside. Igor says that's just his friend, the Count. Beanie Boos usually stop asking questions once they hear that!

Inky

R
Outrageous Ocean
Animal:
Octopus

PERSONALITY: Logical

FAVORITE FOOD: Seaweed salad

LOVES: Solving equations

DISLIKES: Accidently inking herself when she gets embarrassed

ENJOYS: Writing math problems in the sand

RIVAL MATH GROUP: The Calculus Crustaceans

PERSONAL POEM:
I'll spray ink if you get close,
And it'll really stain your clothes!

BIRTHDAY: March 24

Not only is Inky supercute, she's supersmart! Her favorite subject is math, and she's the president of the Mighty Mollusks Math Club. She can solve eight math problems at a time using each of her eight arms!

Isla

PERSONALITY: Outgoing

FAVORITE FOOD OR DRINK:
Tutti-frutti tropical slushies

LOVES: Her best friends
fur-ever!

DREAMS OF: Becoming
a makeup artist

LITTLE KNOWN FACT: She has a
closet just for dress-up clothes.

ENJOYS: Running along the ocean
at dawn

PERSONAL POEM:
I like to hang out with my friends
    and play dress-up.
It's fun doing hair and putting on makeup!

BIRTHDAY: May 11

All About Me!

Isla loves hanging out with her Best Furry Friends
(or BFFs!). She hosts island-themed sleepovers
where she and her friends slurp fruity drinks,
play beach games, and sleep with the windows
open to hear the ocean all night long.

Izabella

PERSONALITY: Bright

FAVORITE FOOD OR DRINK: Rainbow sno-cones

LOVES: Racing through the snow

HOBBY: Making colorful snow paintings

SECRET TALENT: Tie-dyeing

BEST FRIEND: Pellie the cat

PERSONAL POEM:
Rub my ears and pet my head.
I will ride the paths, you steer
the sled.

BIRTHDAY:
April 3

Every winter, Beanie Boos look forward to Izabella's Rainbow-Light Winter Night Rides. She decorates her dogsled with colored lights and drives guests for magical rides all through town!

Izzy

Sunny Savannah
Animal:
Zebra

PERSONALITY: Edgy

FAVORITE DRINK: Soda pop

LOVES: Loud music

SIGNATURE HAIRSTYLE: A black Mohawk

LITTLE KNOWN FACT: One of her stripes is a tattoo.

FAVORITE ROCK SONG:
"Welcome to the Jungle"

PERSONAL POEM:
I'm a wild zebra, so hard to train.
I spend my life on the African
plain!

BIRTHDAY:
September 16

Izzy is a rebellious zebra with a love of heavy metal. She has her own electric guitar and plays gigs for all her friends. Her music style isn't for everyone, but Izzy likes to say, "That's just how I rock 'n' roll."

Izzy

Izzy lives in Friendly Field with tons of beautiful plants and flowers. She's an expert gardener and helps the plants grow big and strong. If you look closely, you may just spot her watering each and every flower with her tiny ladybug watering can.

All About Me!

PERSONALITY: Caring

FAVORITE FOOD OR DRINK: Raspberries

LOVES: Gardening

FAVORITE FLOWER:
Daisies

FAVORITE HOLIDAY:
Earth Day

ENJOYS: Whispering secrets to the flowers

PERSONAL POEM:
Helping flowers grow is my biggest duty.
They get real big and show off their beauty.

BIRTHDAY: July 18

Jewel

Rare. Elusive. Mysterious. This is how the Beanie Boos describe Jewel. She lives high up in the Mystic Mountains but no one knows for certain where. If you're lucky enough to spot her, you're in for a rare treat: She'll tell your fortune using her gemstone crystal ball!

PERSONALITY: Elusive

FAVORITE FOOD OR DRINK: Ruby-red grapefruit

LOVES: Mysticism

WOULDN'T: Trade her jewel-toned fur for anything

FAVORITE SCENT: Patchouli

PRIZED POSSESSION: An amethyst gemstone collar

PERSONAL POEM:
They say a leopard can change its spots.
But in my case . . . NOT!

BIRTHDAY: March 14

All About Me!

Jinxy

DISLIKES: Superstitions

SECRETLY: Hums her own theme song wherever she goes

SIDEKICK: Squeaker the mouse

PERSONAL POEM:
Never cross a mean black cat.
They are scarier than a rat!

PERSONALITY: Unlucky

FAVORITE FOOD OR DRINK: Candy apples

LOVES: Superhero comics

BIRTHDAY: October 13

Jinxy may be a black cat, but she's not bad luck! She pretends to be a superhero called Bat Cat and runs around town helping Boos out of sticky situations. Nine times out of ten she winds up breaking a mirror or knocking over a ladder. But that's just a coincidence.

Joey

RMLC

Fantastical Forest
Animal:
Fox

PERSONALITY: Sleek

FAVORITE FOOD OR DRINK: Figs

LOVES: New trends

FAVORITE SEASON: Winter

DISLIKES: Hot weather

CUTEST ACCESSORY: A pink-and-purple muff

PERSONAL POEM:
I am the coolest fox, they call me Joey.
I have the best traction when it's snowy!

BIRTHDAY:
August 13

Foxes don't come any cooler than Joey. She's trendy and chic and has a way of making any fad look fashionable, even purple-gloved paws!

Julep

PERSONALITY: Inventive

FAVORITE FOOD OR DRINK:
Sugar beets

LOVES: Concocting new drinks

DISLIKES: When people
sugarcoat things

SIGNATURE DRINK: Mint Julep
Mango Tango

KNOWN FOR: Making her friends
sweet-treat smoothies on
Valentine's Day

PERSONAL POEM:
I'm totally bananas over you.
It's really, really, really true!

BIRTHDAY:
February 1

Julep is quite the mixologist when it comes
to inventing sugary drinks. Her creative
concoctions are all based on one secret
ingredient: sweet syrup from the rare
Jungle Julep tree!

Junglelove

RMC
Jazzy Jungle
Animal:
Giraffe

PERSONALITY: Lovey-dovey

FAVORITE FOOD OR DRINK:
Candy kisses

LOVES: Falling in love

ENJOYS: Candlelit dinners for two

KNOWN FOR: Saying sweet
nothings

HOBBY: Rose gardening

PERSONAL POEM:
I'm a romantic giraffe, I surely think.
Even my body is red and pink!

BIRTHDAY:
February 7

While making a batch of Valentines,
Junglelove accidently got red paint all
over her fur! But the spots reminded her
of red rose petals, so she decided to
never wash them off.

Kacey

PERSONALITY: Friendly

FAVORITE FOOD OR DRINK:
Eucalyptus tea

LOVES: Hosting parties

KNOWN FOR: Being one
of the most welcoming
animals in the forest

SAYS: "G'day, mate!"

SPECIAL DISH: Veggie Leaf
Wraps

PERSONAL POEM:
Leaves are always my favorite treat.
I even like them better than meat!

BIRTHDAY: February 13

All About Me!

Koalas don't come any friendlier than Kacey.
She's always ready to give someone a big hug
or invite them to one of her famous veggie
barbecues, where all the food is served on
yummy leaves!

Kiki

PERSONALITY: Flashy

FAVORITE FOOD: Spinach

LOVES: Photography

STYLE: Pink bows and manicured toes

DISLIKES: Bad lighting

FAVORITE MAGAZINE: *Glamour Cat*

PERSONAL POEM:
My friends all call me Kitty Kitty
Because they say I'm so pretty
    pretty!

BIRTHDAY: August 16

This pretty kitty can't help smiling for photos wherever she goes. She loves the camera, and her friends say the camera loves her!

King

RMC
Jazzy Jungle
Animal:
Lion

PERSONALITY: Regal

FAVORITE FOOD OR DRINK: Afternoon tea and biscuits

LOVES: Greeting his loyal subjects

FAVORITE SPOT: His king-sized bed

KNOWN FOR: A mighty roar

ENJOYS: Going on royal tours of the jungle

PERSONAL POEM:
I love to give a mighty roar,
Once or twice and
    sometimes more!

BIRTHDAY: September 21

King is the king of the jungle, but not just because he's a lion. He's actually royalty! He's fifth in line to the Beanie Boo crown. He spends his day practicing regal waves and giving speeches.

Kipper

PERSONALITY: Protective

FAVORITE FOOD OR DRINK: Vegemite

LOVES: Playing with her baby

BABY'S NAME: Joey

GREATEST JOY: Watching her little one grow

FAVORITE LULLABY: "Hop-a-Bye, Baby"

PERSONAL POEM:
My baby must stay close to home
Until she is old enough to safely roam!

BIRTHDAY: January 28

All About Me!

Kipper is an awesome mother. She's always playing games with her baby, like hopscotch and double Dutch jump rope. But she's very protective of her little one, and when it's time to head home, the tiny tyke hops right in her pouch!

Kiwi

Kiwi lounges by the pool in the Iridescent Islands all day, soaking up the sun and sipping on fly-tai mocktails. Sometimes they give her indigestion. But to her, it's worth it.

PERSONALITY: Chilling

FAVORITE FOOD OR DRINK: Kiwis

LOVES: The island life

SIGNATURE STYLE: A lily pad–printed beach towel

WOULD NEVER: Choose the pond over the pool

DREAMS OF: Owning her own island

CATCHPHRASE: Burp!

BIRTHDAY: Summertime

All About Me

Kooky

PERSONALITY: Shy

FAVORITE FOOD OR DRINK:
Eucalyptus salad

LOVES: Quiet time

FAVORITE HANGOUT: Her
hammock high in a eucalyptus
tree

KNOWN FOR: Giving her friends
Vegemite sandwiches

CATCHPHRASE: I come
from a land down under.

PERSONAL POEM: None—
Kooky's not really into poetry.

BIRTHDAY:
It's a mystery!

Kooky is a little bit shy when it comes to her
birthday. She doesn't like attention, and she
won't even tell her best friends when her
birthday is.

Lala

R M
Fabulous Farm
Animal:
Lamb

PERSONALITY: Dreamer

FAVORITE FOOD OR DRINK:
Whipped cream

LOVES: Watching the clouds go by

DREAMS OF: Opening a theme
park named La La Land

FAVORITE PASTIME: Romping
through fields of poppies and
petunias

MOTTO: Dream on!

PERSONAL POEM:
The sunny pasture's where I play,
Eating grass throughout the day!

BIRTHDAY: May 21

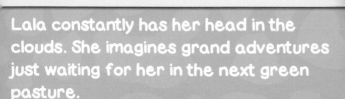

Lala constantly has her head in the
clouds. She imagines grand adventures
just waiting for her in the next green
pasture.

Lavender

PERSONALITY: Relaxed

FAVORITE FOOD OR DRINK:
Cucumber-infused water

LOVES: Luxurious bubble baths

MAKES: Her own essential oils

KEEPS: A lavender-scented baggie
under her pillow

MOTTO: Just relax.

PERSONAL POEM:
I love my purple cute, soft color.
Hold me close, I'm like no other!

BIRTHDAY:
April 15

Lavender is all about relaxation. She has her own salon called Lovely Lavender Day Spa, where Beanie Boos line up for her signature treatment: Fresh Flower Facials.

LeeAnn

PERSONALITY: Stylish

FAVORITE FOOD OR DRINK:
Raspberry tarts

LOVES: Shopping for the latest
jungle style

ADMIRES: Her older brother.
He's her hero.

PRIZED POSSESSION:
A pair of sparkly pink earmuffs

FAVORITE FASHION TREND:
Jungle grass skirts. *So* chic.

PERSONAL POEM:
I like to play with my brother
   who's older.
We roll on the snow hills when it
   gets colder!

BIRTHDAY: December 5

LeeAnn adores staying stylish. Her stripes are the perfect shade of raspberry pink, and she can be a little haughty. But she looks up to her older brother, and he reminds her to stay humble.

Legs

PERSONALITY: Curious

FAVORITE FOOD OR DRINK:
Oyster crackers

LOVES: Treasure hunting

**SECRETLY HOPES SHE'LL
FIND:** The crown jewels!

HER MOM SAYS: Not all
treasure is silver and gold.

FAVORITE BOOK:
Treasure Island

PERSONAL POEM:
I swim down to take a peek
At ocean treasures buried deep!

BIRTHDAY: October 17

All About Me!

Legs fancies herself a Beanie Boo pirate! She spends her days scouring the ocean floor for buried treasure. Her best find? A seashell treasure chest filled entirely with bubble pearls!

R M L C

Jazzy Jungle
Animal:
Leopard

Leona

All About Me!

PERSONALITY: Twinkling

FAVORITE FOOD OR DRINK: Avocados

LOVES: Keeping the party going!

TALENT: Decorating

MOTTO: Light it up!

SPECIAL PARTY DRINK: Blueberry Slushies

PERSONAL POEM:
For I am the prettiest cat,
With bright-green eyes and spots
   to match!

BIRTHDAY: November 18

Leona lives high in a beautiful jungle hut she designed herself. It's covered from floor to ceiling with twinkling green and blue leaf lights to match her fur. She loves hosting Jungle Jamborees for all her friends.

Leyla

RM
Mystic Mountains
Animal:
Sheep

PERSONALITY: Sprightly

FAVORITE FOOD OR DRINK:
Buttercups

LOVES: Frolicking in green valleys

SECRET HIDEOUT: A hollow log
by a babbling mountain brook

FAVORITE MONTH: May

MOTTO: Climb every mountain!

PERSONAL POEM:
One more reason for you to keep:
In 2015 it is the year of the sheep.

BIRTHDAY:
February 18

Springtime is Leyla's favorite time of
year. She climbs mountain slopes to
where the grass is soft and dewy. There
she munches on tender buttercups, her
favorite tasty treat.

Lindi

RM
Fabulous Farm
Animal:
Cat

PERSONALITY: Quiet

FAVORITE FOOD: Corn on the cob

LOVES: A good catnap

PREFERS: To blend in
rather than stand out

FAVORITE SPOT: A tall oak tree
where the sunlight filters through
the leaves just right

HOBBY: Chasing butterflies

PERSONAL POEM:
I'll be your kitty, please cuddle
    with me.
Best friends forever,
    together we'll be!

BIRTHDAY:
May 17

Lindi is a soft-spoken tabby cat who wanders
around the farm and takes naps in pockets
of sunshine. She mostly keeps to herself,
but she gives the coziest cuddles ever.

95

Lizzie

PERSONALITY: Daredevil

FAVORITE FOOD: Papaya

LOVES: New challenges

ALWAYS: On the move

DISLIKES: Sloths

FAVORITE THING: The view from the top

PERSONAL POEM:
I'm the coolest leopard that you will
    ever see.
And you can always find me sitting
    in a tree!

BIRTHDAY:
September 21

Lizzie is a tree-climbing expert. She scales even the most slippery trunks to reach the top of the jungle canopy. In fact, she holds the Beanie-Boo world record for climbing the tallest tree!

London

RMLC
Marvelous
Metropolis
Animal:
Dog

PERSONALITY: Creative

FAVORITE FOOD OR DRINK:
Mystery meat

LOVES: Writing mysteries

TALENT: Sniffing out a good story

MOTTO: It's elementary!

FAVORITE BOOK: *Sherlock Hound*

PERSONAL POEM:
You all will know how much I care
Because I follow you everywhere!

BIRTHDAY: July 18

London likes to imagine she's a mystery writer. If you see her following you, she'll insist it's because she likes you. But really, she's tracing your steps, trying to find inspiration for her next novel!

Lovesy

R Marvelous Metropolis Animal: Dog

Lovesy is just a tiny puppy who has a lot to learn about the world. She'll wag her tail as she explores someplace new, but you can be sure she's holding on tight to her lovey: a little pink stuffed elephant named Ethel.

PERSONALITY: Wide-eyed

FAVORITE FOOD OR DRINK: Apricots

LOVES: Sniffing new things

NEVER GOES WITHOUT: Her lovey

STAYS CLOSE TO: Her mommy

IMAGINES: Being a big dog one day!

PERSONAL POEM:
Let's take a walk all through the park.
We'll play catch from dawn till dark.

BIRTHDAY: October 8

All About Me!

Lucy

Lucy is the gatekeeper to the magical unicorns' home in the Fantastical Forest. She keeps a keen eye out for visitors and hoots at them as they arrive. If you want to get past, you'll have to answer her three riddles!

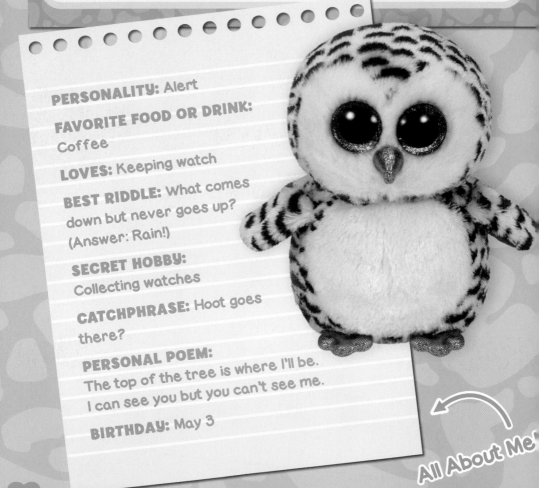

PERSONALITY: Alert

FAVORITE FOOD OR DRINK: Coffee

LOVES: Keeping watch

BEST RIDDLE: What comes down but never goes up? (Answer: Rain!)

SECRET HOBBY: Collecting watches

CATCHPHRASE: Hoot goes there?

PERSONAL POEM:
The top of the tree is where I'll be.
I can see you but you can't see me.

BIRTHDAY: May 3

All About Me

Mac

R M
Marvelous
Metropolis
Animal:
Mouse

PERSONALITY: Mischievous

FAVORITE FOOD: Gingerbread

LOVES: Christmas Eve

DISLIKES: Cats

SECRET HIDING PLACE: Inside Christmas presents

LIVES IN: A gingerbread house in the attic

PERSONAL POEM:
You won't hear me walking when
    I'm in the house
'Cause I'm a tricky and sneaky,
    cute little mouse.

BIRTHDAY:
December 12

If you leave cookies and milk out for Santa on Christmas Eve, watch out! This sneaky little mouse may just sneak them away. Mac can't keep his paws off Christmas treats.

Maddie

R M C
Marvelous
Metropolis
Animal:
Dog

PERSONALITY: Pretty

FAVORITE FOOD OR DRINK: Strawberry dog biscuits

LOVES: Dressing up

DISLIKES: Dirt

LITTLE KNOWN FACT: She has a twin sister, Maggie, who's her complete opposite.

FAVORITE ACCESSORY:
A sparkly pink bow

PERSONAL POEM:
Everyone thinks that I am so cute.
I prefer a dog treat instead of
    fruit!

BIRTHDAY:
March 28

With her pink eyes and puppy-dog nose, Maddie is cute as a button. She's definitely into dainty things, like daisies and dresses and flowers and fairies.

Magic

PERSONALITY: Magical

FAVORITE FOOD: Gumdrops

LOVES: Casting spells

FAVORITE COLOR: Purple

BEST SPELL:
Bippidy-boo, rain go away.
Sun come out so my friends can
    play!

SECRET: Don't tell anyone, but she gets her magical power from her sparkly mane, not her horn!

PERSONAL POEM:
Everyone loves my pretty pink fur.
And casting spells is fun for sure!

BIRTHDAY:
September 20

Magical sparkles float through the air whenever Magic is around. This pink unicorn is famous for casting spells that turn raindrops into rainbows.

Mandy

PERSONALITY: Lovable

FAVORITE FOOD OR DRINK:
Candied bamboo

LOVES: Giving hugs

KNOWN FOR: Writing secret
Valentines

SPECIAL TALENT: Weaving hearts
out of bamboo shoots

WOULD NEVER:
Break anyone's heart

PERSONAL POEM:
I'm not like the other bears.
I have an extra heart I wear!

BIRTHDAY: February 13

Mandy was born with a pink birthmark around her eye in the shape of a heart. Perhaps it's because she's so lovable, just one normal heart wouldn't do!

Mandy

PERSONALITY: Friendly

FAVORITE FOOD OR DRINK: Blueberries

LOVES: Swimming

DISLIKES: Gossip

HOBBY: Making friends

MOTTO: It's what's inside that counts!

PERSONAL POEM:
My favorite time to have lots of fun
Is when I can run and play in the sun.

BIRTHDAY: March 8

All About Me!

Mandy is famous for her blue fur. There's no other poodle quite like her! She's proud of her bright color, but she also knows there's much more to Beanie Boos than what's on the outside.

Maple

No matter where Maple may roam, this proud little moose calls Canada home. He's spirited and spunky and loves to explore the Great White North. If you come to visit, he'll welcome you with some maple cookies and ketchup chips.

PERSONALITY: Welcoming

FAVORITE FOOD OR DRINK: Maple syrup

LOVES: Playing hockey

FAVORITE HOLIDAY: Canada Day

CATCHPHRASE: Eh?

FAVORITE SONG: "O Canada"

PERSONAL POEM:
Canada is our country
Celebrating 150 years of freedom, strength, and diversity.

BIRTHDAY: July 1

All About Me!

Midnight

PERSONALITY: Determined

FAVORITE FOOD OR DRINK: Mini marshmallows

LOVES: Flying school

LITTLE KNOWN FACT: He was born at the stroke of twelve.

FAVORITE COLOR: Black

BEST FRIEND: Jinxy

PERSONAL POEM:
My flying skills are really kinda sad.
I need to practice flapping a tad!

BIRTHDAY: October 30

Flying comes naturally to most bats, but not to Midnight. He flaps and flaps, but just can't get off the ground.

Midnight

PERSONALITY: Naughty

FAVORITE FOOD OR DRINK: Orange jelly beans

LOVES: Silly antics

FAVORITE HALLOWEEN PARTY GAME: Flapping for apples

EARLIEST MEMORY: Learning to tell time

HIS MOM TELLS HIM: It's all fun and games until someone's late for school.

PERSONAL POEM:
When the moon comes out at night
I fly all around but stay out of sight!

BIRTHDAY: January 15

Midnight mayhem is this owl's specialty. He flies around while everyone is fast asleep and resets their clocks to 12 a.m. When they wake up in the morning, they think it's still the middle of the night!

Mist

Mist is a friendly ghost who loves hanging out with his friends. Granted, they don't always know he's there. But sometimes they suddenly see him in the mirror behind them, and *then* they do.

PERSONALITY: Soft-spoken

FAVORITE FOOD OR DRINK: Steamed milk

LOVES: Fog

DISLIKES: Air purifiers

DISTANT COUSIN: Casper

CATCHPHRASE: Didn't mean to scare you.

PERSONAL POEM:
Seeing a ghost is a real scary sight.
But don't be alarmed, I'm not much of a fright.

BIRTHDAY: October 15

All About Me!

Moonlight

PERSONALITY: Mystical

FAVORITE FOOD OR DRINK: Witches' brew

LOVES: Charms and potions

SECRET TALENT: Broomstick flying

PRIZED POSSESSION: His book of spells

FAVORITE SONG: "Dancing in the Moonlight"

PERSONAL POEM:
Casting spells is always fun.
If you're nice, I'll teach you one!

BIRTHDAY:
October 31

Moonlight lives with a kindly old witch who's taught him how to cast spells. But his magic only works when there's a full moon, and he likes to call it Moon Magic!

Muffin

PERSONALITY: Scrumptious

FAVORITE FOOD: Mini muffins

LOVES: The smell of fresh-baked bread

TALENT: Making welcome baskets filled with muffins

PRIZED POSSESSION: A muffin recipe from her great-grandmother

SECRET: She knows the Muffin Man.

PERSONAL POEM:
My pink ear makes me a unique kitty.
And my white fur just looks so pretty!

BIRTHDAY:
January 7

Muffin loves baking every muffin flavor imaginable. She's always trying out different recipes, but her friends have only one thing to say when they try her creations: Yum!

Myrtle

PERSONALITY: Leisurely

FAVORITE FOOD OR DRINK: Slow-cooked oatmeal

LOVES: Taking her time

DISLIKES: Rush hour

FAVORITE PLACE: Myrtle Beach

SECRET TALENT: Rhyming

PERSONAL POEM:
My fancy pink shell looks so great.
But I'm a little slow, so I might be late!

BIRTHDAY: May 25

Try as she may, Myrtle is always running late. Even when she sets her watch ahead ten minutes, she still runs ten minutes behind.

Nacho

RMC
Marvelous
Metropolis
Animal:
Chihuahua

PERSONALITY: Zesty

FAVORITE FOOD OR DRINK: Ghost-pepper salsa

LOVES: Spicing things up

SECRET TALENT: Eating contests

KNOWN FOR: His traveling food truck

FAVORITE HOLIDAY: Cinco de Mayo

PERSONAL POEM:
Eating burritos is always nice.
They're even better with a little spice!

BIRTHDAY: July 18

Nacho is not yo' ordinary dog. He likes things spicy, and he cranks up the cayenne to eleven whenever he cooks. His signature dish? Nacho's Macho Flaming Burritos.

Neptune

Neptune may live under the sea, but she has her head in outer space! Her biggest dream is to soar in a rocket ship around all the planets, starting with her favorite, Neptune!

All About Me!

PERSONALITY: Adventurous

FAVORITE FOOD OR DRINK: Sea-salt caramels

LOVES: Exploring

DREAMS OF: Becoming an astronaut

HOBBY: Collecting space rocks

IN HER DOWNTIME: She enjoys reading Roman mythology.

PERSONAL POEM:
Will you come swim with me
Deep down under the sea?

BIRTHDAY: May 18

Nibbles

Nibbles will never say no to a tasty snack. He can make a whole meal out of finger foods! But don't expect that to fill him up. No matter how much he eats, he always has room for seconds.

All About Me!

PERSONALITY: Hungry

FAVORITE FOOD OR DRINK: Cheese and crackers

LOVES: Vending machines

NEVER LEAVES HOME WITHOUT: His snack pack

BAD HABIT: Talking with his mouth full

DREAM VACATION: An all-you-can-eat cruise

PERSONAL POEM:
There's nothing better than to have a snack.
When I see food I'm on the attack!

BIRTHDAY: February 8

North

RM
Awesome Arctic Animal: Penguin

PERSONALITY: Steadfast

FAVORITE FOOD OR DRINK: Granola bars

LOVES: Compasses

FOLLOWS: The North Star

SKILL: Swimming really fast

MOTTO: Don't stop till you've reached the top!

PERSONAL POEM:
Skating the ice or play in the snow,
Watch how fast I really go!

BIRTHDAY: January 4

When North was just a young chick, his father told him, "Go north, young penguin!" North has been heading north ever since! He won't stop until he reaches the North Pole!

Nugget

R
Fabulous Farm Animal: Chick

PERSONALITY: Darling

FAVORITE FOOD OR DRINK: Puffed wheat

LOVES: Hopping around

SILLY HABIT: Cheeping at bunny rabbits

ADORES: When people stroke his soft feathers

SLEEPS: Curled up in a fluffy yellow ball

PERSONAL POEM:
I may be a little chick but I am very strong.
Tie a ribbon around my neck and I will sing a song!

BIRTHDAY: June 17

The farm is always brighter when Nugget is hopping around. He cheers everyone up with his adorable cheep, cheep, cheeps! He picks up food with his beak, beak, beak!

Olga

Olga is the youngest lamb in her family . . . of over one hundred sheep! She has sixty-four brothers and thirty-five sisters. With a family that large, she has a lot of love to go around.

PERSONALITY: Loving

FAVORITE FOOD OR DRINK: Clover cupcakes

LOVES: Her older brothers and sisters

HOBBY: Knitting wool socks

FAVORITE ACTIVITY: Frolicking with her family

LOOKING FORWARD TO: Her birthday

PERSONAL POEM:
One more reason for you to keep:
In 2015 it is the year of the sheep.

BIRTHDAY: February 18

All About Me

Olive

RMLC
Awesome Arctic
Animal:
Penguin

PERSONALITY: Salty

FAVORITE FOOD: Green olives

LOVES: Proving a point

TALENT: Ice skating

HOPES TO: Learn ice dancing

WHAT'S HOLDING HER BACK: She needs to find an agreeable partner.

PERSONAL POEM:
In the Arctic I love the cold weather. I skate on the ice and spin like a feather!

BIRTHDAY:
October 25

Olive likes to do things her own way, and she can get impatient when other Beanie Boos don't get her ideas. She's not trying to be disagreeable. She just knows she's right.

Ollie

RMC
Outrageous Ocean
Animal:
Octopus

PERSONALITY: Playful

FAVORITE FOOD OR DRINK: Saltwater taffy

LOVES: Finding her friends when they hide

DISLIKES: That her bright pink color makes it hard for *her* to hide

FAVORITE GAME: Hide-and-seek

CATCHPHRASE: Ollie, Ollie, oxen free!

PERSONAL POEM:
Among the pink coral I like to hide In the blue ocean just under the tide!

BIRTHDAY:
January 31

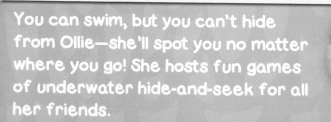

You can swim, but you can't hide from Ollie—she'll spot you no matter where you go! She hosts fun games of underwater hide-and-seek for all her friends.

Opal

RLG
Iridescent Islands
Animal:
Owl

PERSONALITY: Bubbly

FAVORITE FOOD OR DRINK:
Grapefruit fizzy soda

LOVES: Tropical sunrises

TALENT: Jewelry making

DREAMS OF: Opening her own
jewelry boutique

MOTTO: Live colorfully.

PERSONAL POEM:
Have you ever seen colors like this?
Green and gold is
hard to miss!

BIRTHDAY:
July 6

Not many owls live on the Iridescent
Islands, but with her bold, tropical
colors, Opal feels at home there. She
likes searching for beach pebbles to
make into jewelry for her friends!

Orchid

R
Friendly Field
Animal:
Sheep

PERSONALITY: Hopeful

FAVORITE FOOD OR DRINK:
Fruit tarts

LOVES: Listening to birds sing

ENJOYS: Easter egg hunts

FAVORITE DAY: The first day
of spring

FAVORITE PASTIME: Rolling
down grassy hills

PERSONAL POEM:
I like to listen to all the birds sing.
And the best time to do that is in
early spring!

BIRTHDAY:
April 16

Orchid is happiest in warm weather. She
counts down the days until spring. When
she hears birds sing, she knows spring is
right around the corner!

Oscar

Oscar is a true night owl. He soars silently through the dark sky, the moonlight twinkling off his periwinkle feathers. He enjoys dipping in and out of shadows and surprising his friends with a well-timed hoot!

PERSONALITY: Stealthy

FAVORITE FOOD OR DRINK:
Dark chocolate

LOVES:
Solar eclipses

KNOWN FOR: Playing pranks on his friends

SPECIAL TALENT:
Night fishing

FAVORITE PLACE:
His cozy nest inside an ancient tree

PERSONAL POEM:
I like to hunt fish, but only at night.
A real tricky task with only moonlight!

BIRTHDAY: June 10

All About Me!

Owen

Owen used to be a snowy-white owl until one fateful day when he played rainbow tag with his friends. He flew through a vibrant rainbow, and the colors stuck to his feathers! When he isn't playing games, Owen soars over the mountain trees and admires the fall colors.

All About Me!

PERSONALITY: Happy-go-lucky

FAVORITE FOOD OR DRINK: Apple cider

LOVES: When the leaves change colors

SECRET WISH: He wouldn't mind his feathers changing to autumn colors, too!

FAVORITE GAME: Rainbow tag

CATCHPHRASE: Owl catch you later!

PERSONAL POEM:
I like to fly high above the trees
And feel the crisp, cool autumn breeze!

BIRTHDAY:
September 12

Owlette

PERSONALITY: Wise

FAVORITE FOOD OR DRINK: Hoot chocolate

LOVES: Curling up with a good book

FAVORITE HANGOUT: The library

ENJOYS: Sharing fun facts with his friends

MOTTO: Keep calm and read on!

PERSONAL POEM:
Tuck me in to sleep at night.
But when you hug me, hold me tight.

BIRTHDAY: April 20

Owlette always has his beak in a book. He lives in a tree house, where his room looks like a giant library.

Owliver

RMLC Fantastical Forest Animal: Owl

PERSONALITY: Know-it-all

FAVORITE FOOD OR DRINK: Wise Pies (his own recipe!)

LOVES: Knowledge

CHALLENGES HIMSELF WITH: Crosswords and puzzles

PLANS TO: Write a book containing everything he knows

CATCHPHRASE: Let me explain that to you.

PERSONAL POEM:
Over the trees and out of sight,
Owls take flight at midnight!

BIRTHDAY: July 10

Owliver's a bit of a know-it-all. He teaches a General Wisdom class in the forest where he explains things like, "Why is the sky blue?" and "Who's the smartest Beanie Boo on Earth?" (Spoiler: It's him!)

Pablo

PERSONALITY: Tricky

FAVORITE FOOD OR DRINK:
Quesadillas

LOVES: Festivals

SPECIAL DANCE MOVE:
The Chihuahua Cha-Cha

EARLIEST MEMORY: Playing
fetch with his dad

KNOWN FOR: Attracting a crowd

PERSONAL POEM:
If you give me some love, I'll do a trick.
I like to play fetch, just toss me a stick!

BIRTHDAY: June 21

All About Me!

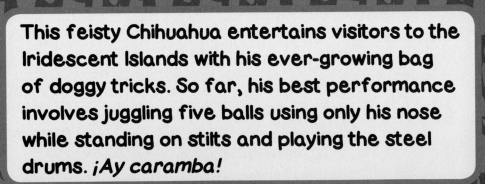

This feisty Chihuahua entertains visitors to the
Iridescent Islands with his ever-growing bag
of doggy tricks. So far, his best performance
involves juggling five balls using only his nose
while standing on stilts and playing the steel
drums. *¡Ay caramba!*

Paddles

PERSONALITY: Fun-loving

FAVORITE FOOD OR DRINK: Raspberry ice pops

LOVES: Splashing

KNOWN FOR: Hosting great parties

PRIZED POSSESSION: His grandfather's canoe

ENJOYS: Just chilling

PERSONAL POEM:
I jump in puddles with my two big
    feet.
Splashing around is
    such a treat!

BIRTHDAY: April 14

Everyone looks forward to Paddles's famous Paddling Pool Parties in the Awesome Arctic. You'd think the water would be too chilly, but Paddles has a secret: All the pools are heated!

Pashun

R
Iridescent Islands
Animal:
Dog

PERSONALITY: Sparkling

FAVORITE FOOD OR DRINK: Strawberry shortcake

LOVES: Lazy island mornings

CRUISE SHIP NAME: *The Pink Lady*

COLLECTS: Pink seashells

NEVER: Feels blue

PERSONAL POEM:
I am precious, friendly, and
    really pink.
The perfect companion for you,
    don't you think?

BIRTHDAY: February 1

Pashun runs a pink sunset cruise off the shore of the Iridescent Islands. The cruise starts with pink lemonade, and then guests enjoy pink spaghetti with pink cotton candy for dessert.

Patches

PERSONALITY: Sneaky

FAVORITE FOOD OR DRINK: Birthday cake

LOVES: Surprising her friends

PRIZED POSSESSION: A patchwork quilt her mom made her

SECRET TALENT: Sign language

CATCHPHRASE: Surprise!

PERSONAL POEM:
I walk around the jungle ground. You can't hear me, I make no sound!

BIRTHDAY: June 5

Patches is the queen of surprises. She surprises her friends with Boo-rrific birthday parties. She surprises her family with unexpected visits. And she'll surprise you with a hug as you stroll through the jungle!

Patsy

PERSONALITY: Prim and proper

FAVORITE DRINK: Pink lemonade

LOVES: A new hairstyle

ENJOYS: Reading fashion magazines

KNOWN FOR: Always lending an ear to her friends

PERSONAL POEM:
Play with me and fluff my hair. I'll sit very quietly on a chair!

BIRTHDAY: May 9

Patsy works at the Pretty Paws Beauty Salon, and all the Beanie Boos know to come to her for perfectly primped fur. She enjoys listening to her customers' stories as much as she likes making them look stylish.

Patty

Awesome Arctic Animal: Penguin

All About Me!

PERSONALITY: Sociable

FAVORITE FOOD OR DRINK: Ice cream cake

LOVES: Playground games

PRIZED POSSESSION: Her friendship bracelet

BEST FRIEND: Glider

FAVORITE GAME: Pat-a-cake

PERSONAL POEM:
Making friends is always nice,
And skating carefully on the ice.

BIRTHDAY: November 18

Patty is the most popular penguin on the Arctic playground because she knows how to play all the wintry recess games. She can skip snowflake rope. She can glide through ice-floe hopscotch. But her favorite game is penguin pat-a-cake!

Peanut

They say an elephant never forgets, and in Peanut's case, it's totally true—because she has a photographic memory! She can remember dates and facts out of a textbook after reading them just once. She aces her tests easy-peanutzy.

PERSONALITY:
Memorable

FAVORITE FOOD OR DRINK: Almond butter

LOVES: History

NEVER FORGETS: Her friends' birthdays

COLLECTS: Traveling trunks

KNOWN FOR: Having an excellent memory

PERSONAL POEM:
Some people think I'm a little bit small.
But one day soon I'll be strong and tall!

BIRTHDAY: March 22

All About Me!

Pegasus

PERSONALITY: Lofty

FAVORITE FOOD OR DRINK:
Golden Delicious apples

LOVES: Starlight

KNOWN FOR: Keeping secrets

ALWAYS: Wears white

FAVORITE STORIES: Mythology

PERSONAL POEM:
I have a gold horn and my fur is
   all white.
These bright colors make it hard
   to hide in the night!

BIRTHDAY:
November 12

Pegasus is only half unicorn. Her other
half is—you guessed it—Pegasus! She can
materialize a golden pair of wings and
fly through the starry sky. How magical is
that?

Pellie

PERSONALITY: Sassy

FAVORITE FOOD OR DRINK: Fruit
punch

LOVES: Being silly

ENJOYS: Blowing raspberries

HER MOM SAYS: If you keep
making that funny face, it might get
stuck that way!

BEST FRIEND: Izabella

PERSONAL POEM:
I like making funny faces.
Then I hide in secret places.

BIRTHDAY:
February 28

Pellie is a sassy cat who will make funny
faces at her friends, and then hide
before they can catch her. She says
she's just being silly.

Penny

RMC
Mystic Mountains
Animal:
Panda

PERSONALITY: Kind

FAVORITE FOOD OR DRINK: Bamboo ice cream

LOVES: Lending an ear

HER FRIENDS SAY: Penny is number one in our book!

ENJOYS: Counting her pennies.

SECRET HOBBY: Coin collecting

PERSONAL POEM:
Just between me and you,
My favorite snack is delicious bamboo!

BIRTHDAY: September 2

A penny for your thoughts. That's what Penny tells her friends whenever they seem down. She's always willing to offer advice, but she'll never give her two cents without being asked!

Pepper

RMC
Friendly Field
Animal:
Cat

PERSONALITY: Misfortunate

FAVORITE FOOD OR DRINK: Peppers

LOVES: Soft tissues

DISLIKES: Allergies

BEST FRIENDS: Firefighters

KNOWN FOR: Constantly sneezing!

PERSONAL POEM:
I sometimes climb up in a tree,
But climbing down is hard for me!

BIRTHDAY: October 8

Ah-choo! That's all Pepper can say because she's always sneezing. Combine that with her habit of getting stuck up trees, and everyone agrees: This little kitty could use a hug.

Petunia

With her pretty pink ears and fluffy purple fur, Petunia is the fanciest bunny ever. She loves playing dress-up and is famous for hosting tea parties in the Friendly Field, where all the guests must wear tutus.

All About Me!

PERSONALITY: Fancy

FAVORITE FOOD OR DRINK: Pastries

LOVES: Pressed flowers

PRIZED POSSESSION: Her collection of frilly party dresses

MOTTO: Don't be afraid to get fancy!

TALENT: Weaving crowns out of petunias

PERSONAL POEM:
I'm the fanciest bunny in the world, I think.
My body's purple and my ears are pink!

BIRTHDAY: February 24

123

Phantom

PERSONALITY: Spooky

FAVORITE FOOD OR DRINK:
Unknown

LOVES: Whispering

DISLIKES: Ghost hunters

RUMOR HAS IT: He lives in a
hollowed-out tree in the mountains

CATCHPHRASE: Listen.

PERSONAL POEM:
Haunting houses is always nice.
I'll scare you once or maybe twice!

BIRTHDAY:
October 31

What's that whispery sound? Is it just the
wind, or could it be . . . Phantom? This eerie
ghost haunts cabins and is rarely seen, but
his ghostly *ooooooooooooos* can be heard
whistling through open windows.

Pierre

PERSONALITY: Charming

FAVORITE FOOD OR DRINK:
Grilled peaches

LOVES: When people bring him food

SECRET TALENT: Batting his eyes
just right to get what he wants

RUMOR HAS IT: His fur turned
pink from lying in the sun too long!

FAVORITE SEASON: Summer

PERSONAL POEM:
I build sandcastles on the beach,
While I nibble on a peach!

BIRTHDAY:
January 22

Pierre may look innocent, but he's a total charmer who
knows how to get his way! With a few bats of his eyes, he
can convince his pals to come play with him.

Piggley

Piggley is the most unusual pig you'll ever meet—because he likes things tidy and neat! He doesn't mind playing with his friends as long as it's in the grass or hay. But when they start splashing in the mud, Piggley stays far away.

PERSONALITY: Neat and clean

FAVORITE FOOD OR DRINK: Broccoli

LOVES: Keeping organized

FAVORITE PASTIME: Folding clothes and matching socks

ALWAYS: Colors within the lines

DISLIKES: When people call his home a sty

PERSONAL POEM:
I like to roll, hop, and play
When all my friends jump
in the hay!

BIRTHDAY: March 8

All About Me!

Pinky

Fabulous Farm Animal: Owl

If flowers could talk, they'd say Pinky is their best friend. She waters her flower garden each day, sings to her posies, and makes sure they have just the right amount of sunlight. But she would never pick her flowers—that would be rude!

PERSONALITY: Beautiful

FAVORITE FOOD OR DRINK: Strawberries

LOVES: Growing flowers

ENJOYS: Pink sunsets

HOBBY: Painting flowers on teacups

MOTTO: Everything looks pretty in pink.

PERSONAL POEM:
If you look up in the night sky
You just may see me flying by!

BIRTHDAY: August 14

All About Me

126

Piper

PERSONALITY: Musical

FAVORITE FOOD OR DRINK: Blueberry pie

LOVES: Playing her flute

DISLIKES: Discord

TALENT: She has perfect pitch.

FAVORITE STORY: *The Pied Piper*

PERSONAL POEM:
I'm a pretty fox with nice pink ears. So stay my friend throughout the years!

BIRTHDAY: April 6

When Piper plays her flute, it's music to everyone's ears! She's a master musician who leads the Beanie Boos' wind ensemble.

Pipper

PERSONALITY: Protective

FAVORITE FOOD OR DRINK: Starfruit

LOVES: Starry nights

DISLIKES: Clouds covering the moon

HEADS TO BED: At sunrise

SITS ON: A branch high up in a pear tree

PERSONAL POEM:
When I sit in a tree late at night, The stars shine big and bright!

BIRTHDAY: November 13

Pipper soars around the Fabulous Farm at night keeping an eye on all the sleeping animals. Her soft hoots often lull them to sleep.

Pippie

One magical day on the Fabulous Farm, a white fluffy cloud floated down from the sky. When it lifted, there was Pippie! This precious pooch isn't sure if he was born up in the clouds or just got carried away by one, but he's determined to go back up there one day!

PERSONALITY: Airy

FAVORITE FOOD OR DRINK: Puffed marshmallows

LOVES: Watching the clouds roll by

WHEN HE GROWS UP: He wants to be a pilot

WEIRD FACT: He never remembers his dreams. They're always foggy when he wakes up.

WANTS TO MEET: Halo the bear

PERSONAL POEM:
My eyes are big and filled with love.
You're my heavenly star that fell from above.

BIRTHDAY: March 20

All About Me

Pixy

PERSONALITY: Festive

FAVORITE FOOD: Funnel cake

LOVES: Carnivals

FAVORITE RIDE: Ferris wheel

FAVORITE HOLIDAY:
Mardi Gras

HOBBY: Trying on wacky
costumes

PERSONAL POEM:
At carnivals I ride the Ferris
   wheel,
Then play some games and eat
   a meal!

BIRTHDAY:
May 26

Pixy's horn is truly magical. Not only can it change color, but she can use it to make glittering fireworks, too! The Beanie Boos love the magical fireworks displays she sets off at carnivals.

Pokey

PERSONALITY: Nosy

FAVORITE FOOD OR DRINK:
Seaweed noodles

LOVES: Being in the know

HIS FRIENDS SAY: Pokey should
mind his own business.

SECRET TALENT: A keen sense of
hearing

CATCHPHRASE: What's the buzz?

PERSONAL POEM:
I like to swim around the sea.
The coral reef is home to me!

BIRTHDAY: May 25

Pokey pokes around the coral reef all day, noodling through other Beanie Boos' business. Maybe it's just because he's bored. But nobody likes a busybody!

129

Posy

RM
Fabulous Farm
Animal:
Chick

PERSONALITY: Wide-eyed

FAVORITE FOOD: Jelly beans

LOVES: Everything! It's all brand-new to her!

SAYS: Peep, peep, peep!

LITTLE KNOWN FACT: Her mom leaves a trail of jelly beans for Posy to follow back to the barn each night.

BEST FRIEND: Goldie

PERSONAL POEM:
I eat jelly beans almost every day.
They're my favorite
  treat I have to say!

BIRTHDAY:
February 25

This wide-eyed little chick is fresh on the farm and can't wait to celebrate her first Easter. Her mom even filled her basket with shimmery pink grass to jump in!

Precious

RM
Marvelous
Metropolis
Animal:
Dog

PERSONALITY: Always happy

FAVORITE FOOD OR DRINK: Trifle

LOVES: Curling up in her doggy bed

WOULD NEVER: Turn down a walk in the park

FAVORITE GEMSTONE: Pink quartz

BEST MEMORY: Her birthday trip to the beach

PERSONAL POEM:
I am smart and happy and bright pink.
The perfect pet for you, don't you think?

BIRTHDAY:
August 19

Precious is a one-in-a-million puppy. She's smart, she's happy, she's kind, and she gets along with everyone. What's not to love?

Presents

Presents gives the best gifts at the holidays because she takes the time to think about what each and every one of her friends loves the most. But the Beanie Boos agree: Her friendship is the greatest gift of all!

PERSONALITY: Generous

FAVORITE FOOD OR DRINK: Peppermint bark

LOVES: Wrapping gifts

FAVORITE HANGOUT: Under the Christmas tree

MOST MEMORABLE GIFT: A handmade scrapbook filled with memories

FAVORITE HOLIDAY GAME: Secret Santa

PERSONAL POEM: I stay warm in the snow for sure, Thanks to my red hat and brown fur!

BIRTHDAY: December 17

All About Me!

Princess

PERSONALITY: Imaginative

FAVORITE FOOD: Bonbons

LOVES: Tales of knights in shining armor

WEARS: A dress-up tiara to school

ALWAYS: Treats her friends with royal kindness

BELIEVES: One day my prince will come!

PERSONAL POEM:
I always love such pretty things,
Like my pink hairdo and diamond rings!

BIRTHDAY:
January 8

When Princess was little, her mom would read her the story of Sleeping Beauty before bedtime. Princess liked to imagine that *she* was a real princess, and she always went to sleep with sweet dreams!

Pugsly

PERSONALITY: Affectionate

FAVORITE FOOD OR DRINK:
Egg rolls

LOVES: HUGS

ASKS HIS PARENTS:
Can I have a hug?

ASKS HIS FRIENDS:
Want a hug?

ASKS HIS CLASSMATES:
Who's ready for a group hug?!

PERSONAL POEM:
Lift me up and give me a hug,
And you'll make me a happy pug!

BIRTHDAY:
September 22

Pugsly LOVES hugs. He'll hug everything and everyone. His friends. His family. Trees. There's something about a good old hug that puts a smile on his face.

Rainbow

All About Me!

PERSONALITY: Colorful

FAVORITE FOOD OR DRINK:
Rainbow ice pops

LOVES: Bright colors

HOBBY: Collecting prisms

DOESN'T: Let things get her down

MOTTO: You need a little rain in order to have a rainbow.

PERSONAL POEM:
My pretty colors match oh so well.
And my magic horn can cast a spell!

BIRTHDAY: May 3

If you look up in the sky and see a rainbow arcing through the mountains, you can bet Rainbow is behind it. Her magical horn can create rainbows out of thin air, and what's more, they're Riding Rainbows. That means all her friends can slide down them!

Rainbow

PERSONALITY: Colorful

FAVORITE FOOD OR DRINK: Confetti cake

LOVES: Taking selfies with her friends

SECRET DREAM: To be a celebrity hairstylist!

DISLIKES: Humid weather

MOTTO: Be you. There's no one like you!

PERSONAL POEM:
They call me Poofie because of my hair.
It has style and flair and it's the coolest
   to wear.

BIRTHDAY: May 3

All About Me!

Rainbow never has a bad hair day . . . because her hair is enchanted! Her soft poodle curls shimmer with all the colors of the rainbow, and rumor has it, petting her will bring you good luck.

Razberry

PERSONALITY: Swinging

FAVORITE FOOD OR DRINK:
Raspberry jam

LOVES: Swing dancing

ENJOYS: When Beanie Boos give her sweet compliments

DON'T: Sniff her dance shoes. They stink!

WISHES: Romeo the gorilla would be her dance partner. He's so dreamy!

PERSONAL POEM:
My name is Razberry and I'm
    especially sweet
Except for the smell of my two
    stinky feet!

BIRTHDAY:
April 16

The Razzle-Dazzle Dance Studio is where you'll find Razberry the monkey. She's got moves you've never seen!

Reagan

PERSONALITY: Dramatic

FAVORITE FOOD: Cherries jubilee

LOVES: Acting

LITTLE KNOWN FACT: Her name is inspired by Regan from Shakespeare's *King Lear*.

EVEN LITTLER KNOWN FACT: She didn't like that *King Lear* was a tragedy, so she restaged it as a comedy!

ALWAYS: Casts her friends in her plays

PERSONAL POEM:
I'm such a pretty kitty, pink
    and blue.
And when I pick
    friends, I
    pick you!

BIRTHDAY:
November 13

Drama is Reagan's middle name—as in, Shakespearean drama. She's a wonderful actress and can tackle any role, whether it's from a comedy or a tragedy.

Rebel

R M C
Sunny Savannah
Animal:
Meerkat

PERSONALITY: Rebellious

FAVORITE DRINK: Cherry cola

LOVES: Motorcycle racing

KNOWN FOR: Walking on the wild side

SIGNATURE STYLE: A leather jacket

FAVORITE MOVIE: *Rebel Without a Cause*

PERSONAL POEM:
My African home is very nice.
I've even seen lions
once or twice!

BIRTHDAY:
May 19

Rebel is a daredevil always on the lookout for the next big adventure, and if you hear a motorcycle race revving through the savannah, that's probably his doing.

River

R M
Fantastical Forest
Animal:
Wolf

PERSONALITY: Free-flowing

FAVORITE FOOD: River trout

LOVES: Seeing where life takes her

RUMOR HAS IT: She accidently rolled in paint one day and the colors looked so good on her fur, she just went with it.

PRIZED POSSESSION:
A river-rock sculpture

MOTTO: Easy goin', easy flowin'.

PERSONAL POEM:
She'll get around to writing one someday.

Like a rolling river, River rolls wherever life takes her. She's just as happy to go on a countrywide road trip as she is to relax at home in her wolf lodge.

Rocco

Rocco is a sneaky Beanie Boo bandit who enjoys snatching things from his friends when they aren't looking! But he always gives the treasures right back. To him, the fun part is seeing what he can get away with!

All About Me!

PERSONALITY: Sneaky

FAVORITE FOOD OR DRINK: Moon pies

LOVES: Shiny things

SECRET HIDEOUT: A hollowed-out log in the Fantastical Forest

KNOWN FOR: Peering out from the shadows with his huge eyes

HATES: Getting caught!

PERSONAL POEM:
I like the night more than the day,
So we'll have fun in wacky ways!

BIRTHDAY: February 27

137

Romeo

PERSONALITY: Hopeless romantic

FAVORITE FOOD: Banana muffins

LOVES: Sonnets

SECRET CRUSH: Razberry

WHY HE DOESN'T TELL HER: Their families don't really get along.

FAVORITE AUTHOR: Shakespeare

PERSONAL POEM:
I eat bananas right off the tree.
The jungle life is good for me!

BIRTHDAY:
December 31

Romeo spends his days swinging from tree to tree, thinking deep thoughts. His biggest secret is that he's in love, but until he works up the courage to tell his crush, he'll just write romantic Personal Poems about her.

Rootbeer

PERSONALITY: Fizzy

FAVORITE FOOD OR DRINK:
Root beer floats

LOVES: New ice cream flavors

ENJOYS: Playing Frisbee in the park

FAVORITE ICE CREAM FLAVOR:
Peanut-butter crunch

FAVORITE ACTIVITY:
Riding in the ice cream truck

PERSONAL POEM:
I love to run and jump and play.
I like to catch Frisbees every day!

BIRTHDAY:
December 26

Rootbeer knows the Marvelous Metropolis Ice Cream Parlor is the place to be. They have all his favorite treats: the Caramel Swizzle Sundae, the Banana Split Smoothie, and, of course, their root beer floats!

Rosey

Shimmering Sky Animal: Unicorn

Rosey is the one and only Beanie Boo Sky Ballerina. She magically floats and twirls in the air using her enchanted ballet slippers. And sometimes, she even makes it rain sparkles during the encore.

PERSONALITY: Graceful

FAVORITE FOOD OR DRINK: Rose hip tea

LOVES: Roses

SIGNATURE BALLET MOVE: The Prancing Pirouette

PRIZED POSSESSION: Her magical ballet slippers. They were a gift from a kindly enchantress.

LITTLE KNOWN FACT: She choreographed her own ballet!

PERSONAL POEM:
I like to dance in the sky.
The magic happens when I fly!

BIRTHDAY: August 7

All About Me!

Rosie

R Outrageous Ocean
Animal: Turtle

PERSONALITY: Cheerful

FAVORITE FOOD OR DRINK: Hibiscus iced tea

LOVES: Roses

EARLIEST MEMORY: Hatching out of a purple-speckled shell

FAVORITE GAME: Playing I Spy in the coral reef

PRIZED POSSESSION: Her underwater flower garden

PERSONAL POEM:
I am pink and purple and swim happily.
My shell's covered with roses for you to see!

BIRTHDAY: November 4

Rosie's a super sunny sea turtle. The only thing Rosie enjoys more than cheering up her friends is a big bouquet of fresh flowers!

Roxie

RMC Mystic Mountains
Animal: Raccoon

PERSONALITY: Bold

FAVORITE FOOD OR DRINK: Watermelon rinds

LOVES: That her bright, jewel-toned look stands out at night

UNEXPECTED OUTCOME: Those bright colors make it hard for her to blend in!

FAVORITE TIME OF DAY: Nighttime

MOTTO: Rock on.

PERSONAL POEM:
I scavenge for food all through the night.
But as soon as its daylight I'll be out of sight!

BIRTHDAY: February 18

Roxie is totally rocking. She is the DJ of the Beanie Boos' band, Bear Tracks. She loves getting her paws in the mix!

Ruby

RMC
Iridescent Islands
Animal:
Monkey

PERSONALITY: Daredevil

FAVORITE FOOD OR DRINK:
Mangoes

LOVES: Pushing things to the limit

DISLIKES: Rules

WOULD NEVER: Accept a
time-out

CATCHPHRASE: None of
the regular rules apply.

PERSONAL POEM:
I swing the trees
As much as I please!

BIRTHDAY:
August 23

When it comes to rules, Ruby has no rules.
She stays out past her bedtime. She eats
breakfast for dinner. She even swings from
the highest island palm tree branches just to
prove she can!

Rusty

R
Marvelous Metropolis
Animal:
Raccoon

PERSONALITY: Resourceful

FAVORITE FOOD OR DRINK: He'll
eat anything . . . anything!

LOVES: Scavenging for food

KNOWN FOR: His infamous
garbage stew

DISTANTLY RELATED TO: Rocco
the raccoon

PERSONAL POEM:
I know it's stinky, but it's true.
I really love my garbage stew.

BIRTHDAY: July 11

Some Boos turn up their noses at Rusty,
since his garbage stew is so smelly. But
Rusty doesn't mind. He's proud of his
cooking skills, and he'll share his stew
with any Boos who ask.

141

Safari

PERSONALITY: Spunky

FAVORITE FOOD OR DRINK: Tossed salad

LOVES: Standing on high ledges, looking out over the savannah

DREAMS OF: Climbing Mount Kilimanjaro

FAVORITE SPORT: Basketball

MOTTO: Who you callin' "short"?

PERSONAL POEM:
I can see skies of blue or a little field mouse.
After all, I have the best seat in the house!

BIRTHDAY: October 20

All About Me!

Whatever you do, don't call Safari "short." She may be tiny as far as giraffes go, but she's got big ideas, even bigger dreams, and nothing keeps her from standing tall!

Sami

PERSONALITY: Forgetful

FAVORITE FOOD OR DRINK:
Orange-flavored ice pops

LOVES: His sea anemone home

CAN'T HELP: Clowning around

**WEIRDEST PLACE HE'S GOTTEN
LOST:** Inside the stomach of a whale!

BEST FRIEND: Aqua the fish

PERSONAL POEM:
The coral reef is where I play.
I'm fun and cute is
    what they say!

BIRTHDAY:
January 22

Sami is a lovable little clownfish with a habit
of getting lost in the coral reef. It's not his fault—sometimes
he just gets carried away while playing hide-and-seek! His
friends can usually spot him by his bright-orange fins.

Sammy

PERSONALITY: Rowdy

FAVORITE DRINK: Root beer

LOVES: Western movies

SECRET TALENT:
Country line dancing

FAVORITE BAND:
Hootie and the Boo Fish

SECRET TALENT: Ventriloquism

PERSONAL POEM:
I live in the meadow, way up in
    a tree.
I hoot all night, but you can't see me!

BIRTHDAY:
June 12

This rootin', tootin' owl can't stop hooting!
He used to live in the Fantastical Forest,
but all his hooting was keeping everyone
awake, so now he lives in a tall oak tree in
the meadow.

143

Sandy

PERSONALITY: Environmentalist

FAVORITE FOOD OR DRINK: Krill sandwiches

LOVES: Protecting the environment

DISLIKES: Littering, waste, and oil spills

FAVORITE DAY: Earth Day

MOTTO: The Earth is our home, so we have to take care of it!

PERSONAL POEM:
I'm a sea turtle from the troubled
 Gulf Coast.
My wild friends and I need your help
 the most.

BIRTHDAY: May 18

Sandy loves her sea home so much, it makes her sad to think it could be in danger. So she makes sure to remind everyone how precious it is. Her friends want to protect the sea, too.

Sapphire

R
Sunny Savannah
Animal:
Zebra

PERSONALITY: Wild

FAVORITE DRINK: Fruit punch

LOVES: Doing acrobatics

BEST MOVE: The Zany Zebra Backflip

MOTTO: Walk on the wild side.

BEST FRIEND: Treasure the unicorn. They're two crazy peas in a pod.

PERSONAL POEM:
My stripes are pink, my mane is
 green.
I'm the wildest zebra you've
 ever seen!

BIRTHDAY:
January 30

This vibrantly colored zebra can do all sorts of wild and crazy acrobatics, and when she's around, you know the party is going to get funky.

Scarem

R
Fantastical Forest Animal: Bat

Deep in the Fantastical Forest stands a towering castle that Scarem calls home. His friends have never been there. There's a rumor he has a closet filled with dark cloaks. But why would a bat need that?

PERSONALITY: Dark and mysterious

FAVORITE FOOD OR DRINK: Blood oranges

LOVES: Counting

DISLIKES: The sun

FAVORITE BOOKS: Gothic thrillers

SECOND LANGUAGE: Romanian

PERSONAL POEM:
My fangs are very sharp and real.
Watch out, or you'll be my next meal!

BIRTHDAY: October 11

All About Me!

145

Scoop

RM
Awesome Arctic Animal:
Snowman

FAVORITE CHRISTMAS SONG:
"Frosty the Snowman"

MOTTO: Just roll with it.

PERSONALITY: Joyful

FAVORITE FOOD OR DRINK:
Chocolate cherries

LOVES: Snowball fights

ENJOYS: Ice skating

PERSONAL POEM:
I'm a giant snowball with a big
 heart of gold.
And I love playing outside when
 it's real cold.

BIRTHDAY: January 5

Some snowmen get a frosty attitude when it's below zero, but not Scoop. This chillaxin' snowman just rolls with the punches. In fact, he rolls everywhere. It's kind of his thing.

Scoops

RM
Awesome Arctic Animal:
Snowman

LOVES: Sledding

PERSONAL POEM:
I like the taste of cocoa when I'm
 froze,
But I can't smell it much with my
 carrot nose!

PERSONALITY: Jolly

FAVORITE FOOD: Candy canes

KNOWN FOR BEING:
Light and fluffy

BIRTHDAY:
December 25

Whoever said no two snowflakes are alike must have been thinking about Scoop and Scoops. They're complete opposites! One likes candy canes, the other chocolate cherries. One likes ice skating, the other sledding. Don't even *think* about calling them twins.

Scooter

R
Friendly Field
Animal:
Snail

Scooter is an easygoing, go-with-the-flow snail who scoots along at her own pace. The larger Boos can usually spot her bright colors in the tall grass, but occasionally she'll blend in with the garden flowers and almost get squished!

PERSONALITY: Laid-back

FAVORITE FOOD OR DRINK: Garden veggies

LOVES: Soft meadow breezes

FAVORITE TIME OF YEAR: Harvest season

MOTTO: Slow and steady wins the race.

DISLIKES: Large feet!

PERSONAL POEM:
In the garden, I'm a busy snail.
Nibbling all day on tasty kale!

BIRTHDAY: February 15

All About Me!

Scraps

Don't throw those table scraps away—Scraps will eat them! He's a hungry dog and doesn't mind leftovers. In fact, they're his favorite meal!

All About Me!

PERSONALITY: Scrappy

FAVORITE FOOD OR DRINK: Leftovers

LOVES: Seeing what's for dinner

HOME: A doghouse behind a deli

ALWAYS: Wags his tail when the deli-shop back door opens

WOULD NEVER: Let good food go to waste

PERSONAL POEM:
I live behind a deli shop.
I eat hot dogs and drink soda pop!

BIRTHDAY: January 11

Serena

PERSONALITY: Elusive

FAVORITE FOOD OR DRINK: Pink potion lemonade

LOVES: Spells

FAVORITE COLORS: Pink and purple

WOULD LIKE TO:
Get out and meet more friends

FAVORITE BOOK:
The Lord of the Rings

PERSONAL POEM:
I have pink eyes and spots of pink.
Can we be friends? What do you
　　think?

BIRTHDAY:
June 3

Serena is a quiet leopard tucked away in the Mystic Mountains. Some Beanie Boos think she's a wizard's apprentice learning magical spells. It's even said that her spots used to be black, but she used magic to turn them pink and purple.

Shadow

PERSONALITY: Shady

FAVORITE FOOD OR DRINK:
Butterscotch candies

LOVES: Shadowing people

FAVORITE HANGOUT: A dark alley behind a haunted house

HER FRIENDS SAY: She's not really mean . . . right?

MOTTO: Never cross a black cat.

PERSONAL POEM:
It might be scary to look in my eyes.
They're darker and meaner than
　　the night skies.

BIRTHDAY:
October 17

Shadow uses superstitions to her advantage. She shadows trick-or-treaters with her little basket, and they'll usually give her as much candy as she wants to make her go away.

Shelby

PERSONALITY: Grateful

FAVORITE FOOD OR DRINK:
Sand-dollar pancakes

LOVES: Her beautiful pink shell

SECRET HANGOUT: A small
sandbar along the shore

FAVORITE TIME OF DAY: Sunrise
on the ocean

BELIEVES: Wishes really do
come true!

PERSONAL POEM:
I'm the prettiest turtle in the sea.
My pink shell looks good on me!

BIRTHDAY:
February 21

Shelby used to admire the rainbowy inside
of the oyster shells she'd spot under the sea. She wished
her shell could look that beautiful, too. Then, one day, she
made a wish upon a magical sea star, and lo and behold,
her wish came true!

Sherbet

PERSONALITY: Silly

FAVORITE FOOD: Sorbet

LOVES: Clowning around

DISLIKES: Frowns

TALENT: Doing somersaults

SILLY TRICK: She can fit in a tiny
car . . . along with a dozen other
puppies.

PERSONAL POEM:
I'm a happy dog when you're
    around,
But sometimes I act like a clown!

BIRTHDAY:
February 8

Sherbet dreams of running off to join the
circus! She just knows she has what it takes
to be a clown. Her friends say that if she
did, she'd be the cutest clown in the ring.

Skylar

All About Me!

PERSONALITY: Mystifying

FAVORITE FOOD OR DRINK:
Lavender crêpes

LOVES: Meteor showers

SECRET: Even Skylar doesn't
know where she came from.

NOT A SECRET: She wants to
make as many friends as possible!

LITTLE KNOWN FACT: When she
feels like it, she can glow in
the dark.

PERSONAL POEM:
It's no secret that I intend
To give you hugs and be your friend!

BIRTHDAY: November 20

No one really knows where Skylar came from.
One night, there were lots of twinkling lights
floating down from the heavens. And suddenly,
Skylar appeared! Some say she's an alien
unicorn. Others say she came from a star.
Skylar says she's just herself.

Ⓡ

Awesome Arctic
Animal:
Husky

Skylar

Skylar is the best cook in the Great White North. His burgers are the best and his beef stew is out of this world. His secret? He doesn't use beef at all—he uses tofu!

PERSONALITY: Tender

FAVORITE FOOD OR DRINK: Tofurkey

LOVES: Culinary masterpieces

TALENT: Inventing new recipes

ENJOYS: Family-style meals

DREAM: To meet master chef Gordon *Ram*-say

PERSONAL POEM:
I really love to eat beef stew,
But only if I eat with you!

BIRTHDAY: May 14

All About Me!

152

Slick

PERSONALITY: Sly

FAVORITE FOOD: Sprinkle donuts

LOVES: Running fast

FAVORITE HIDING SPOT: He won't tell!

HIS FRIENDS WONDER: What *does* that fox say?

SECRET TALENT: He has some slick dance moves.

PERSONAL POEM:
I'm sly in the forest, I hide under wood.
A visit from hunters would never be good.

BIRTHDAY: May 1

Slick darts behind trees, keeping out of sight so he can nab snacks from the unicorn Beanie Boos. He doesn't say much, probably because his mouth is always full of tasty treats!

Slowpoke

RMC Outrageous Ocean Animal: Turtle

PERSONALITY: Slow and steady

FAVORITE FOOD OR DRINK: Soufflé

LOVES: Taking her time

DISLIKES: Tailgaters

CATCHPHRASE: I only have one other speed, and it's slower.

ALWAYS: Makes time to stop and smell the roses.

PERSONAL POEM:
I walk with style and grace
At a very, very slow pace!

BIRTHDAY: August 18

Slowpoke may be slow moving, but she's got quick wit. If you tell her to speed it up, she'll quip at you faster than you can say "move out of the way."

153

RMLC
Awesome Arctic Animal: Dog

Slush

Slush is a seriously strong dog, and he's helpful, too! He leads a giant sled that takes everyone where they want to go. He loves snow sports and is training for the Winter Beanie Boolympics!

PERSONALITY: Strong

FAVORITE FOOD OR DRINK: S'mores

LOVES: Cold weather

DISLIKES: Sitting still

HOBBY: Snowboarding

CATCHPHRASE: Snow wonder!

PERSONAL POEM:
Through wind or sleet or rain or snow,
I'll take you where you want to go!

BIRTHDAY: April 30

All About Me!

Smitten

PERSONALITY: Lovable

FAVORITE FOOD OR DRINK: Candy hearts

LOVES: His stuffed bear

WOULD NEVER: Harm a fly (much less eat one)

KNOWN FOR: Giving great hugs

CATCHPHRASE: Ribbit!

PERSONAL POEM:
For the best hug you ever had,
Hop over to my lily pad!

BIRTHDAY:
April 9

Smitten is head-over-webbed-feet for his special someone! He's a loving little froggy who enjoys nothing more than cuddling.

Sophie

PERSONALITY: Playful

FAVORITE FOOD OR DRINK: Bubble gum

LOVES: Blowing bubbles

BEST BIRTHDAY SURPRISE: A piñata filled with gumballs

FAVORITE SPOT: The yard outside the candy store

MOTTO: Just keep poppin'!

PERSONAL POEM:
Meow is what I mostly say.
In the yard is where I play.

BIRTHDAY:
January 13

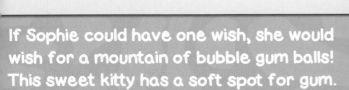

If Sophie could have one wish, she would wish for a mountain of bubble gum balls! This sweet kitty has a soft spot for gum.

Sparkles

When the setting sun streaks the sky with gold and pink, you might spot Sparkles jumping in the waves. But don't blink, or you might miss her! This sparkly dolphin is rumored to be magical and she's always slipping just out of sight.

PERSONALITY: Mysterious

FAVORITE FOOD OR DRINK: Rock candy crystals

LOVES: Pink sunsets

MAGICAL POWERS: It's said she can grant wishes.

PRIZED POSSESSION: A shiny seashell necklace

DISLIKES: Storm clouds

PERSONAL POEM:
I am a dolphin, can't you see?
Jump in the water and swim with me!

BIRTHDAY: November 29

All About Me

156

Speckles

PERSONALITY: Friendly

FAVORITE FOOD OR DRINK:
Gummy flies

LOVES: Lunchtime

FAVORITE GAME: Leapfrog

SITS ON: A speckled log

PERSONAL POEM:
Give me a bug
And I'll give you a hug.

BIRTHDAY:
May 1

Ribbit! That's how Speckles says hello to his friends when they pass his pond. He's an upbeat amphibian who enjoys munching lunch and then hopping into the pool where it's nice and cool.

Speckles

PERSONALITY: Sneaky

FAVORITE FOOD OR DRINK:
Pineapple chunks

LOVES: Sneak-attack hugs

SECRET: He has night vision!

FAVORITE BIRD: The speckled warbler

GOOD TO KNOW: His hugs are like quicksand. You just keep sinking into them!

PERSONAL POEM:
I climb the tree oh so fast.
And then I pounce in a flash!

BIRTHDAY: November 19

Speckles is known for pouncing on his friends with sneak-attack hugs. No one is really crazy about his antics. But a leopard's gotta do what a leopard's gotta do.

157

Specks

PERSONALITY: Squinty

FAVORITE FOOD: Pears

LOVES: Magnifying glasses

DISLIKES: Small print

ALWAYS: Packs her spare pair of glasses

DREAMS OF: Having 20/20 vision

PERSONAL POEM:
This is the day all my dreams will come true—
And all I want is to share them with you.

BIRTHDAY: March 8

Specks has such bad vision, she can barely see her trunk in front of her face. She has glasses, but she hates how they keep sliding down her trunk!

Spells

PERSONALITY: Enchanting

FAVORITE DRINK: Butterbeer

LOVES: Learning new magic spells

LIVES: In a cozy nook under a staircase in a wizard's castle

DREAMS OF: Becoming a famous author

FAVORITE FICTIONAL CHARACTER: Hedwig from Harry Potter

PERSONAL POEM:
My feathers are a snowy white.
They look so good when I take flight!

BIRTHDAY:
July 31

Careful—Spells might put a spell over you! This snowy white owl tells such fascinating stories, he doesn't need magic to do what he does best—make everyone want to listen.

Spike

All About Me!

PERSONALITY: Skittish

FAVORITE FOOD OR DRINK: Mushrooms

LOVES: Scratching his spikes against trees

HIS FRIENDS JOKE: If your hair's a mess, just ask Spike to brush it for you. His spikes make a great comb!

WHEN HE GETS NERVOUS: He curls up in a tight little ball.

AFRAID OF: Badgers

PERSONAL POEM:
My prickly fur stands up so straight.
My digging skills are also great!

BIRTHDAY: April 12

Spike's prickly fur is nothing to be scared of. He's a skittish creature who mostly just minds his own business. But if he does give you a hug, he promises not to poke you. Kind of.

Spirit

R Marvelous Metropolis Animal: Cat

PERSONALITY: Patriotic

FAVORITE FOOD: Apple pie

LOVES: Baseball

HOBBY: Collecting flags

SECRET TALENT: He can name all the presidents!

FAVORITE MEMORY: Singing "The Star-Spangled Banner" at the Beanie Boo Ball Game

PERSONAL POEM:
Red, White, and Blue, you know what it means.
I'm thankful to live in the land of the free!!

BIRTHDAY: May 2

Spirit is proud to call the United States home. He's a stand-up Beanie Boo who does what's right, and knows that freedom isn't free.

Squeaker

R Marvelous Metropolis Animal: Mouse

PERSONALITY: Zippy

FAVORITE FOOD: Cheese

LOVES: Running races

DISLIKES: When people tell him to be quiet

HOBBY: He has a stinky cheese collection

HOME: A clock in the center of town

PERSONAL POEM:
On my tippy toes, I run real fast.
If I'm in a race I'll never come last!

BIRTHDAY: May 3

You'll never miss Squeaker speeding past because he's constantly squeaking! He doesn't mean to be so noisy—but it can be hard sneaking a piece of cheese when you can't stop squeaking.

Stars

R

Fantastical Forest
Animal:
Bear

Once a year, Stars comes out of his forest den to visit the Marvelous Metropolis for its Independence Day celebration. He's thankful for his friends and family, and, most of all, his freedom.

PERSONALITY: Strong-willed

FAVORITE FOOD OR DRINK: Mixed-berry cobbler

LOVES: Backyard parties

ENJOYS: Parades

ADMIRES: Great leaders

BEST FRIEND: Spirit

PERSONAL POEM:
My favorite colors are red, white, and blue.
This means freedom for me and you.

BIRTHDAY: July 4

All About Me!

161

Sting

PERSONALITY: Clever

FAVORITE FOOD: Nectarines

LOVES: Grammar

LITTLE KNOWN FACT: Her grandfather wrote the Beanie Boo Encyclo-*bee*-dia.

PET PEEVE: When people confuse "there," "their," and "they're."

FAVORITE BOOK: The dictionary

PERSONAL POEM:
English class is a piece of cake.
I'm the Spelling Bee champ, for
goodness sake!

BIRTHDAY:
September 24

Sting is the queen bee of reading and writing. She spells every word correctly. Her sentences use perfect grammar. If there's a Spelling Bee she'll be buzzing straight to first place.

Stripes

PERSONALITY: Outrageous

FAVORITE FOOD: Berries

LOVES: To boogie!

FAVORITE DANCE: The Tiger Twist

DOESN'T WORRY ABOUT: What other people think

CATCHPHRASE: Groovy

PERSONAL POEM:
I live in a groovy little jungle hut
Where I dance around and shake
my butt!

BIRTHDAY: February 13

Don't tell this tiger to change her stripes. She's happy just the way she is, living the good life, playing her music on maximum volume, and boogying to the beat.

Sugar

R M
Marvelous
Metropolis
Animal:
Elephant

PERSONALITY:
Sweet

FAVORITE FOOD OR DRINK: Candy-coated nuts

LOVES: Playing board games

DISLIKES: Lemons

DRINKS HER TEA: With six spoonfuls of sugar

MOTTO: Life is sweet.

PERSONAL POEM:
I'm so happy when I'm with you.
I'm never sad, I'm never blue!

BIRTHDAY: February 18

All About Me!

Sugar loves sweets so much, it's all she ever thinks about. She even invented her own board game that takes place in a land filled entirely with candy. Now if only she could think of a name for her game.

R M

Fantastical Forest Animal: Unicorn

Sugar Pie

The mouthwatering scent of pie wafting through the Fantastical Forest means that Sugar Pie is baking! Her pies are simply scrumptious, but she only makes them on the third Tuesday of every other month, so they're a rare treat.

PERSONALITY: Whimsical

FAVORITE FOOD OR DRINK: Shoofly pie

LOVES: Baking from scratch

KNOWN FOR: Baking mini pies for her friends on Valentine's Day

SECRET INGREDIENT: A little bit of love

WOULD NEVER: Use magic for baking. Homemade is best.

PERSONAL POEM:
Valentine's kisses, I'll give them to you.
I'd love to be friends, with you I'll be true!

BIRTHDAY: March 3

All About Me!

164

Surf

RMC
Outrageous Ocean
Animal:
Dolphin

PERSONALITY: Far out

FAVORITE FOOD OR DRINK:
Dried seaweed

LOVES: Catching waves

DISLIKES: Wiping out

BEST FRIEND: Sparkles the dolphin

CATCHPHRASE: Surf's up!

PERSONAL POEM:
My friends and I swim all day.
The ocean is a great place to play!

BIRTHDAY: August 11

Have you ever seen a dolphin surf? Surf is an expert wave rider who can balance on the surfboard using only her tail. Totally radical!

Sweetikins

R
Marvelous
Metropolis
Animal:
Bear

PERSONALITY: Cuddly

FAVORITE FOOD OR DRINK:
Melted chocolate

LOVES: Her grandmother

BEST FEATURE: Her chubby cheeks

HOBBY: Crocheting heart doilies

FAVORITE MEMORY: Visits to her grandma's cottage

PERSONAL POEM:
You'll be forever in my heart.
I promise you, we'll never part!

BIRTHDAY:
March 29

Sweetikins was just a nickname her grandmother called her, but everyone loved it so much, she decided to make it her real name.

Sweetly

Listen close and Sweetly will tell you a tale. A sweet story filled with flower gardens and magic and maybe some Beanie Boo fairies. Could the story be true? Only Sweetly knows for sure.

All About Me!

PERSONALITY: Sweet

FAVORITE FOOD OR DRINK: Sweet peas

LOVES: Fantasy stories

ENJOYS: Singing sweet songs

KNOWN FOR: Sparking her friends' imagination

BELIEVES: There's nothing as sweet as a happy ending.

PERSONAL POEM:
I surely am the sweetest bear.
Here's my heart to show I care!

BIRTHDAY: February 21

Swoops

PERSONALITY: Film fanatic

FAVORITE FOOD OR DRINK: Popcorn

LOVES: Superhero movies

HOSTS: A weekly party called Midnight Movie Madness

SPECIAL TALENT: He draws his own comic books.

INVENTED: His own superhero, Super Bat. He has superpowers *and* a cape.

PERSONAL POEM:
I like to flap across the sky.
All night long I love to fly!

BIRTHDAY: October 30

Swoops is a huge fan of superhero movies. He loves watching the good guys on the big screen, and always cheers when they swoop in to save the day.

Swoops

PERSONALITY: Daredevil

FAVORITE FOOD OR DRINK: Caramel lattes

LOVES: Performing stunts

BEST STUNT: The Double-Winged Loop Swoop

ENJOYS: Night swooping

CATCHPHRASE: I'll swoop you off your feet!

PERSONAL POEM:
My big eyes can see at night.
So I fly around by the moonlight!

BIRTHDAY: September 12

This owl is a total daredevil who performs crazy swooping stunts. Whenever his friends hear his trademark *swoop whoop*, they know to duck for cover!

R M L C

Iridescent Islands
Animal:
Leopard

Sydney

Sydney used to climb a tree a day in the Jazzy Jungle until, one day, she ran out of trees. So she hopped on a boat to the Iridescent Islands and started climbing all the trees there, too!

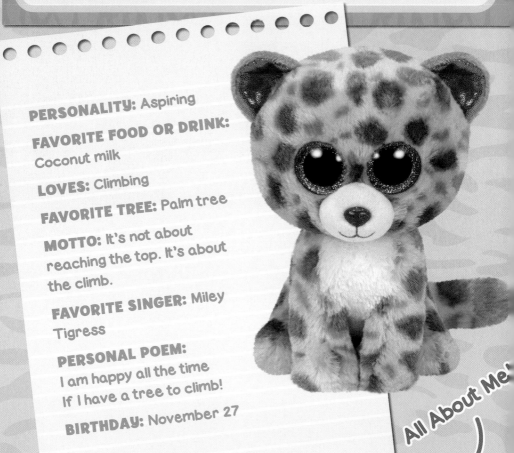

PERSONALITY: Aspiring

FAVORITE FOOD OR DRINK: Coconut milk

LOVES: Climbing

FAVORITE TREE: Palm tree

MOTTO: It's not about reaching the top. It's about the climb.

FAVORITE SINGER: Miley Tigress

PERSONAL POEM:
I am happy all the time
If I have a tree to climb!

BIRTHDAY: November 27

All About Me!

T-Bone

PERSONALITY: Peppy

FAVORITE FOOD: Doggy bones

LOVES: Gnawing on stuff

NEVER: Has a bone to pick with anyone

SECRET MISCHIEF: He sometimes buries his friends' slippers.

CLAIMS TO KNOW: Who let the dogs out

PERSONAL POEM:
I hide and bury bones every day
So you and I can always play!

BIRTHDAY: March 13

Burying things comes naturally to T-Bone. He has a map of all the best spots in town to bury his bones, so that whenever the mood for a game of find the bone strikes, he knows exactly where to go.

Tabitha

PERSONALITY: Collector

FAVORITE FOOD OR DRINK: Broken breadsticks

LOVES: Collecting things

CAN BE FOUND: Poking through yard sales

HOBBY: Freecycling

MOTTO: Your trash is my treasure.

PERSONAL POEM:
I can be your fluffy cat
'Cause I'm so pretty just to look at!

BIRTHDAY: December 17

Tabitha loves collecting weird stuff. Old balls of yarn. Holey socks. Pencil stubs. She swears it's all useful. But for what?

Tala

Tala is the number-one student at Beanie Boo School. She's a straight-A whiz with a knack for sniffing out answers, and she's always eager to help her friends with their homework (as long as she doesn't accidentally eat it first).

PERSONALITY: Smart

FAVORITE FOOD OR DRINK: Pizza

LOVES: Acing a test

DISLIKES: Getting an answer wrong

CAN BE FOUND: Doing homework in the labra-*dor*-y

WORST DREAM: Forgetting to study for her final exams!

PERSONAL POEM:
I'm a smart dog. I can roll over and crawl.
And I will fetch when you throw the ball!

BIRTHDAY: October 9

 All About Me!

Tangerine

RMC
Jazzy Jungle
Animal:
Orangutan

PERSONALITY: Troublemaker

FAVORITE FOOD: Rotten bananas

LOVES: Making mischief

CLASSIC PRANK: Covering mud-filled holes with banana leaves so Beanie Boos accidently slide in!

LIKES TO THINK: The jungle is jazzy because of her.

CATCHPHRASE: I love trouble.

PERSONAL POEM:
Monkey business is what I do.
I swing, I eat, and play around, too!

BIRTHDAY:
November 25

Tangerine is a darling little monkey . . . who loves getting into trouble. Banana peels to throw? Check. As Tangerine likes to say, monkey is her business, and business is good.

Tasha

RMLELC
Jazzy Jungle
Animal:
Leopard

PERSONALITY: Introverted

FAVORITE FOOD OR DRINK:
Chocolate-covered apricots

LOVES: Cooling off in the water

MISSES: Her homeland in the mountains

FAVORITE SEASON: Winter

FAVORITE GAME: Cat's cradle

PERSONAL POEM:
You'll not see me during the day
Because my spots help me to hide away.

BIRTHDAY:
January 4

Tasha came to the jungle all the way from the snowy mountains. She's still getting used to the hot weather. But when the temperature rises, her friends coax her down to the water to cool off.

Tauri

PERSONALITY: Snuggly

FAVORITE FOOD OR DRINK: Warm milk

LOVES: Cuddling

NEVER LEAVES HOME WITHOUT: His stuffed mouse

FAVORITE THING: Warm towels fresh from the dryer

FAVORITE BEDTIME STORY: *The Tale of Tom Kitten*

PERSONAL POEM:
Hear me purr. I don't want to nap.
It's time to be held, so I'll jump in
    your lap.

BIRTHDAY: February 4

All About Me!

Feeling warm and cozy is number one in Tauri's book. He loves to curl up with cuddly blankets and purr. Sometimes he's so busy getting snuggly at bedtime, he forgets to fall asleep!

Tender

PERSONALITY: Heartfelt

FAVORITE FOOD OR DRINK: Chocolate heart candies

LOVES: Linking trunks with her friends

KNOWN FOR: Giving tender hugs

WOULD NEVER: Forget her friends

MOTTO: Hugs are the best way to start the day!

PERSONAL POEM:
There's no elephant as sweet as me.
Hearts even decorate my ears you see!

BIRTHDAY: February 14

Tender has a lovely heart-print pillowcase that she slept with every night. Then, one magical evening, the heart pattern stuck to her ears!

Tess

PERSONALITY: Genius

FAVORITE FOOD OR DRINK: Popcorn. She loves to count the kernels!

LOVES: Math

NAMED AFTER: Tesla the tiger

ENJOYS: Solving brainteasers

EARLIEST MEMORY: Counting to ten

PERSONAL POEM:
There is nothing I wouldn't do
To have a great friend that's just like you!

BIRTHDAY: March 7

Tess is a math whiz. She can add up numbers superfast. She says she developed her love of math as a baby by counting the stripes on her back!

Thankful

R
Friendly Field Animal: Turkey

PERSONALITY: Eager

FAVORITE FOOD OR DRINK: Pumpkin pie

LOVES: Dessert

BAD HABIT: His eyes are WAY bigger than his stomach.

WORSE HABIT: Talking with his mouth full

WHEN HE GOBBLES: It sounds like, *gobbbblliizizz gobbblithfffz gobbbbbbbbrrrrllll.*

PERSONAL POEM:
I eat too much pumpkin pie.
That's the reason I can barely fly!

BIRTHDAY: November 22

At Thanksgiving time, Thankful gobbles up so much pumpkin pie, his mouth is too full to even gobble! But he always remembers to say thank you.

Tinsel

RMLC
Marvelous Metropolis Animal: Owl

PERSONALITY: Leader

FAVORITE FOOD: Figgy pudding

LOVES: Decorating the Christmas tree

KNOWN FOR: Making homemade tinsel

FAVORITE CHRISTMAS CAROL: "O Christmas Tree"

SECRET: He'll sneak into the elves' workshop to peek at the presents.

PERSONAL POEM:
I'm as white as the winter snow.
Wrap me up and tie me in a bow!

BIRTHDAY: December 12

Have you ever heard of Tinsel the Red-Hatted Owl? He has a very important job! When Rudolph the Red-Nosed Reindeer takes a vacation, Tinsel helps guide Santa's reindeer sleigh team through the sky on Christmas Eve.

Tomato

Marvelous Metropolis Animal: Dog

R

PERSONALITY: Saucy

FAVORITE FOOD: Ketchup

LOVES: Chasing red taillights

DISLIKES: When people mispronounce his name. (It's To-MAY-to, *not* To-MAH-to.)

HOBBY: Vegetable gardening

BIRTHSTONE: Ruby

PERSONAL POEM:
If I get lost staying out at night,
You'll always find me 'cause I'm
   so bright.

BIRTHDAY: July 1

All About Me!

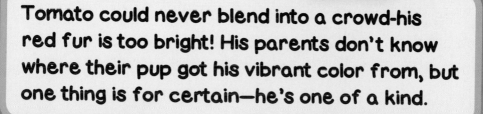

Tomato could never blend into a crowd—his red fur is too bright! His parents don't know where their pup got his vibrant color from, but one thing is for certain—he's one of a kind.

Tracey

You'd never guess it from her cute puppy-dog appearance, but Tracey is a world-renowned dog fashion designer! Her blue bow is trademarked, and the logo on her clothing line is a tracing of her paw print.

PERSONALITY: Chic

FAVORITE FOOD OR DRINK: Pup-tarts

LOVES: Sewing

FASHION LINE: Smart casual

SIGNATURE LOOK: A blue bow

FASHION INSPIRATION: Fields of bluebells

PERSONAL POEM:
I'm the smartest dog of all.
I'll always come by you when you call!

BIRTHDAY: December 7

All About Me!

Treasure

R Sunny Savannah
Animal:
Unicorn

PERSONALITY: Rare

FAVORITE FOOD: Lollipops

LOVES: Treasure hunting

PRIZED POSSESSION: Her rare jewel collection

SECRET SKILL: Sapphire has taught her to do acrobatics!

SAYS: Sapphire is the rarest treasure of all—a best friend.

PERSONAL POEM:
I collect jewels—that's no surprise.
My favorite gems match my eyes.

BIRTHDAY: January 15

Treasure didn't always live in the Sunny Savannah, but then she met Sapphire the zebra, and the two became inseparable friends!

Treats

R Marvelous
Metropolis
Animal:
Ghost

PERSONALITY: Excitable

FAVORITE FOOD OR DRINK: Black jelly beans

LOVES: Trick-or-treating

CARRIES: *Two* baskets for twice the candy

DOESN'T MIND: Sugar highs

NOT REALLY CLOSE WITH: Grimm

PERSONAL POEM:
Let's go out and trick-or-treat.
We'll get some candy that we can eat!

BIRTHDAY:
August 1

Halloween is Treats's favorite night of the year. It's the night when he gets to eat as many treats as he wants—ghosts don't get tummy aches from eating too many sweets!

Trixie

Trixie is the kind of cat who pours milk into her fruity-crisp cereal and swirls it around until it's a rainbow-colored, mish-mash mess. Then she pretends it's a special soup and slurps it all up!

PERSONALITY: Quirky

FAVORITE FOOD OR DRINK: Cereal

LOVES: Brand-new days in the jungle

KNOWN FOR: Creating weird food combos

HER FRIENDS SAY: What *is* that?!

ALWAYS WILLING: To try something new

PERSONAL POEM:
I live among a jungle of green,
The most beautiful place I've ever seen.

BIRTHDAY: November 14

All About Me!

Tuffy

PERSONALITY: Nervous

FAVORITE DRINK: Herbal tea

LOVES: A good night's sleep

SOMETIMES: Has bad dreams

KNOWN FOR: Barking in her sleep

HER FRIENDS KNOW: Her bark is worse than her bite.

PERSONAL POEM:
Some people say I'm not too bright
Because I like to bark and
    sometimes bite!

BIRTHDAY: February 2

Tuffy goes to sleep each night on a tufted pillow made by the Beanie Boo unicorns. It helps Tuffy have pleasant dreams all night so she won't bark in her sleep.

Tundra

PERSONALITY: Welcoming

FAVORITE FOOD: Snow peas

LOVES: Cozy blankets

FEELS MOST AT HOME: When he's surrounded by friends

NEVER LEAVES HOME WITHOUT: His snowshoes

LITTLE KNOWN FACT: His igloo is one of the largest in the Arctic.

PERSONAL POEM:
The ice and snow is all I see.
A frozen igloo is the
    home for me!

BIRTHDAY:
October 12

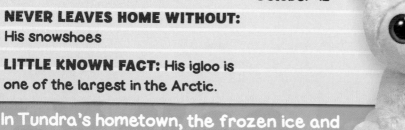

In Tundra's hometown, the frozen ice and snow go on for miles and miles. So he built an awesome igloo home that's warm and cozy, and now all his friends can come to visit.

Tusk

PERSONALITY: Neat and clean

FAVORITE FOOD OR DRINK:
Watercress sandwiches

LOVES: Brushing his teeth

MOTTO: A healthy smile is
a happy smile.

KNOWN FOR: Giving toothy grins

ENJOYS: Swimming to see
his friends

PERSONAL POEM:
In water I go, I have no fear!
It's much more fun than
lying on the pier!

BIRTHDAY:
October 20

Tusk is a tenacious walrus with big dreams of becoming a
dentist. He's had lots of practice cleaning his friends' tusks,
and he never swims anywhere without his toothbrush!

Twiggy

R M
Fantastical
Forest
Animal:
Owl

PERSONALITY: Fashionable

FAVORITE FOOD: Lychees

LOVES: The latest trends

FAVORITE ACCESSORY:
A pair of glittery pink shoes

KNOWN FOR: Ruffling a few
feathers with her fashion blog

MOTTO: Keep it chic.

PERSONAL POEM:
I'm glad to have a friendship
with you.
We can share clothes and
even shoes!

BIRTHDAY:
January 11

Twiggy is the youngest of five owls, so
she's used to sharing everything. But
she doesn't mind. She has a style all her
own and loves sharing her feathery
fashion tips with you.

Twigs

RMC Sunny Savannah
Animal: Giraffe

PERSONALITY: Straightforward

FAVORITE FOOD OR DRINK: Twigs and leaves

LOVES: Reaching the most tender leaves at the very tops of the trees

ENJOYS: Lazy summer afternoons

FAVORITE COLOR: Green

KEEPS: A twig plant in her room for midnight snacks

PERSONAL POEM:
I am friendly, tall, and sweet.
Eating leaves is my favorite treat.

BIRTHDAY: September 4

This cute pink giraffe earned the nickname Twigs because she likes to munch on twigs all day. She's not on a diet—they just taste really good to her.

Twinkle

RMC Fabulous Farm
Animal: Lamb

PERSONALITY: Wishful

FAVORITE FOOD OR DRINK: Sponge cake

LOVES: Looking for wishing stars

WISHES: To go on grand adventures

ALWAYS: Makes one wish before bedtime each night

FAVORITE LULLABY: "Twinkle, Twinkle, Little Star"

PERSONAL POEM:
My home is always on the farm.
It's cozy with its southern charm!

BIRTHDAY: May 11

Of course, a starry-eyed lamb like Twinkle would love wishing upon stars. They're just so magical!

Twinkle Toes

RM
Friendly Field
Animal:
Bunny

PERSONALITY: Light-footed

FAVORITE DRINK: Carrot juice

LOVES: The ballet

FAVORITE DANCE: The *paw-de-deux*

CAN'T HELP: Shopping for new tutus

PRIZED POSSESSION: Her lucky ballet slippers

PERSONAL POEM:
I like to spin on the tips of my toes.
Come and watch, I am the
    star of the show!

BIRTHDAY:
May 12

Twinkle Toes is a star ballerina. She was Clara in the squirrels' production of *The Nutcracker*. Now if only the bunnies would put on a ballet, she'd be happy indeed!

Valentina

R
Mystic Mountains
Animal:
Panda

SECRETLY: Hopes to one day find her special someone

BELIEVES: What good is fashion without someone to impress?

FAVORITE DESIGNER: Valentino

PERSONALITY: Swanky

FAVORITE FOOD OR DRINK: Pink fizz fountain soda

LOVES: Fashion shows

PERSONAL POEM:
I always want to be with you.
And I only hope you love me, too.

BIRTHDAY: February 10

Have you ever seen a panda as fashionable as Valentina? She never has a fur out of place, and she absolutely adores playing dress-up.

Valor

PERSONALITY: Trustworthy

FAVORITE FOOD OR DRINK: Hot dogs

LOVES: Food, family, and friends

DOES: One hundred push-ups every morning

ADMIRES: Other Beanie Boos who have served with him

PRACTICES: His salute in the mirror

PERSONAL POEM:
I'm covered in red, white, and blue.
And to my country I will always be true.

BIRTHDAY: July 3

Valor knows what it means to be a hero. He's rescued twenty-nine kittens stuck up trees. He was awarded a special medal for Beanie Boo Bravery!

Violet

R
Marvelous Metropolis Animal: Leopard

PERSONALITY: Floral

FAVORITE FOOD OR DRINK: Violet-infused ice cream

LOVES: Smelling pretty

TALENT: Playing the clarinet

LEADS: Her school marching band

SHE'S NO: Shy violet

PERSONAL POEM:
My fur is the prettiest in all of the land,
And I'm the best-looking in my marching band!

BIRTHDAY:
June 15

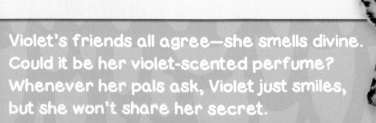

Violet's friends all agree—she smells divine. Could it be her violet-scented perfume? Whenever her pals ask, Violet just smiles, but she won't share her secret.

Waddles

RMLC
Awesome Arctic
Animal:
Penguin

PERSONALITY: Cute and clumsy

FAVORITE FOOD OR DRINK:
Ice cream waffles

LOVES: Going fast

BEST FRIEND: Icy the seal

DANCE MOVE:
The Wobbly Waddle

FAVORITE BOOK: *Mr. Popper's Penguins*

PERSONAL POEM:
When I swim, I go really fast.
But when I run, I'm usually last!

BIRTHDAY:
May 11

Poor Waddles. He just wants to get everywhere as fast as possible, but he can't help tripping over his own two feet.

Warrior

RM
Fantastical
Forest
Animal:
Wolf

PERSONALITY: Robust

FAVORITE FOOD OR DRINK:
Noodles

LOVES: Martial arts

LOOKS UP TO: His great-wolf grandfather

SECRET HIDEOUT: A lodge in the mountains

ENJOYS: Kung Fu movies

PERSONAL POEM:
He doesn't have time for poetry—he's training!

BIRTHDAY: Martial artists never tell their age.

Warrior is a champion mixed martial artist, and he has a black belt in jiujitsu! He never fights for real—only for practice. But he'll ready if bad guys ever came to town!

Wasabi

PERSONALITY: Tricky

FAVORITE FOOD OR DRINK: Banana splits

PRIZED POSESSION: His fancy magician's top hat

FAMOUS FOR: His sleight of paw

FAVORITE SAYING: Magic is something you make

PERSONAL POEM:
My name in the jungle is spunky
  monkey,
And all my tricks are really funky.

BIRTHDAY:
May 18

Wasabi dreams of being a magician someday. When night falls in the Jazzy Jungle, he calls his friends around and performs magic tricks for them. He's getting really good! He can make a banana disappear in about three seconds flat.

Whiskers

PERSONALITY: Loyal

FAVORITE FOOD: Dog biscuits

LOVES: Long walks

CAN'T HELP: Chasing the mailman!

ALWAYS: Makes his friends feel safe

SECRET HOBBY: Bird-watching

PERSONAL POEM:
I never growl, except at
  strangers.
Or to let you know I think there's
  danger!

BIRTHDAY:
March 13

Whiskers is loyal and always watches out for his friends. If he thinks someone's up to no good—watch out! His bark is *not* bigger than his bite!

Wild

PERSONALITY: Wild and crazy

FAVORITE FOOD OR DRINK: Pomegranate juice

LOVES: All-night rave parties

OWNS: Her own jungle club

ORIGINALLY FROM: The island of Ibiza

FAVORITE SONG: "Jungle Boogie"

PERSONAL POEM:
I'm the rarest Zebra you've ever seen
Because my body is purple and green!

BIRTHDAY: January 13

Wild hosts the wildest rave parties in the Jazzy Jungle! The DJs she books are off the hook. Everyone agrees: If you want a wild party, talk to Wild.

Willow

PERSONALITY: Soft

FAVORITE FOOD OR DRINK: Shirley Temples

LOVES: Snuggling

KNOWN FOR: Purring when she's happy

FAVORITE PLANT: Pussy willows

ALWAYS SLEEPS WITH: A fluffy pink pillow

PERSONAL POEM:
I have a pink bow and pretty gray fur.
When you rub my belly, it makes me purr!

BIRTHDAY: January 2

Willow is like a fluffy little puffball who snuggles up to you and gives the cutest nuzzles in the world. Who could resist cuddling with such an adorable kitty?

Wise

PERSONALITY: Wise

FAVORITE DRINK: Ginseng tea

LOVES: Debates

DISLIKES: Wisecrack jokes

LITTLE KNOWN FACT: He gets cold easily—that's why he never leaves home without his scarf.

FAVORITE SCIENTIST:
Nic-*owl*-lous Copernicus

PERSONAL POEM:
I keep my neck warm with my
   scarf on so tight.
It won't even come off when I fly
   through the night!

BIRTHDAY: September 20

Is it wise to have a debate with Wise? Well, that depends on the depth of your knowledge. This clever owl can recite the dictionary forward *and* backward. Can you?

Wishful

RMLC
Shimmering Sky Animal: Unicorn

PERSONALITY: Wishing and dreaming

FAVORITE DRINK: Guava juice

LOVES: When wishes come true

EARLIEST MEMORY: Arriving in the Shimmering Sky on a shooting star

HOBBY: Collecting charm bracelets

FAVORITE NURSERY RHYME:
"Star Light, Star Bright"

PERSONAL POEM:
The best part of being a unicorn
Is giving wishes with
   my magical horn!

BIRTHDAY:
November 10

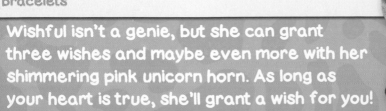

Wishful isn't a genie, but she can grant three wishes and maybe even more with her shimmering pink unicorn horn. As long as your heart is true, she'll grant a wish for you!

Woody

PERSONALITY: Speedy

FAVORITE FOOD OR DRINK: Tender tree bark

LOVES: Munching on sticks

ALWAYS: Offers guests tasty wood chips

HIS DENTIST SAYS: Woody's teeth will never stop growing.

HONORARY MEMBER OF: The Busy Beaver Association

PERSONAL POEM:
Everyone likes my
    soft brown fur.
And I hop so fast
    I'm just a blur!

BIRTHDAY:
April 25

Most rabbits like to chomp on carrots, but Woody prefers to munch on wood. He has a distant relative who's a woodchuck, so maybe that's where Woody gets his appetite from.

Wynnie

PERSONALITY: Easygoing

FAVORITE FOOD OR DRINK: Frozen drinks

LOVES: Beach games

DISLIKES: Long flights

FAVORITE PARTY GAME: The limbo

CATCHPHRASE: Let's party!

PERSONAL POEM:
I relax in places where it is hot.
Let's be friends! Why not?

BIRTHDAY: September 19

Though Wynnie has beautiful wings, he would rather spend his time at a beac party than flying. He's the first one to start a conga line or challenge friend: to a round of limbo!

Yago

PERSONALITY: Free-spirited

FAVORITE FOOD: Fish and chips

FAMOUS FOR: His stealthy flying moves

LIKES: A nice nocturnal flight

DISLIKES: Having his daytime nap interrupted

PERSONAL POEM:
At night, I like to fly the coast.
By day, I always sit on a post.

BIRTHDAY:
June 27

Yago loves his home in the Shimmering Sky. At night, he swoops around visiting friends and admiring the moonlight on the ocean. But come daytime, you can find him sound asleep on his post with his beak tucked firmly under one wing.

Yumi

PERSONALITY: Patient

FAVORITE DRINK: Oolong tea

LOVES: Soft morning breezes

ALWAYS: Listens

HOBBY: Calligraphy

SECRET TALENT: Writing haiku

PERSONAL POEM:
I like to climb the tallest trees
'Cause way up high I eat the leaves!

BIRTHDAY:
August 23

Yumi knows that in order to climb to the treetops, you must be patient. Her friends appreciate her quiet wisdom and often look to her for advice.

Zazzy

PERSONALITY: Quirky

FAVORITE FOOD OR DRINK:
Raspberry tarts

LOVES: Standing out

BEST FRIEND: Bubbly the owl

FAVORITE GAME: Bubbly will fly,
and Zazzy will chase after her

SPECIAL TALENT: Painting
pink line art

PERSONAL POEM:
In a herd of zebras I'm easy to see.
Look for pink stripes and you'll
know it's me!

BIRTHDAY:
August 21

Zazzy is the one and only zebra who lives in
the Fantastical Forest. Why would a zebra
live in the woods? Because she's best
friends with an owl, that's why!

Zig-Zag

PERSONALITY: Constantly flip-
flopping

FAVORITE FOOD OR DRINK:
Cookies and cream

LOVES: Her zigzag stripes

KNOWN FOR: Coming and going

HER FRIENDS SAY: She can
never make up her mind

FAVORITE GAME: Freeze tag
(because she never gets caught!)

PERSONAL POEM:
Wild fur is what you see.
I have crazy stripes
    all over me!

BIRTHDAY:
June 14

How do you catch a zigzagging zebra? You
don't! Zig-Zag is one of the swiftest and most
agile zebras on the savannah.

Zippy

RMLELC
Iridescent Islands
Animal:
Turtle

PERSONALITY: Relaxed

FAVORITE FOOD: Watermelon

LOVES: Floating on the water

DISLIKES: Rushing waves

HOBBY: Yoga

MOTTO: There's so much you miss when you go too quick.

PERSONAL POEM:
I like to swim in the sea for fun.
And then I rest on the beach in
    the sun!

BIRTHDAY:
May 6

When Zippy's parents named him, they had no idea he would be one of the most laid-back, easygoing turtles ever. Zippy would rather spend all day lazing on the rocks than speeding by too quickly.

Zoey

RMC
Sunny Savannah
Animal:
Zebra

PERSONALITY: Zany

FAVORITE FOOD: Cinnamon-sugar-coated French fries

LOVES: Hanging out with friends

EARLIEST MEMORY: Running free in the Serengeti

FAVORITE THING: Her stuffed bear named Toto

WHEN SHE'S AWAY: She misses the rains down in Africa.

PERSONAL POEM:
Hello, I am Zoey, Africa is my home.
My zigzag stripes keep me safe as
I roam!

BIRTHDAY:
April 18

Zoey is a wild and crazy zebra who just can't contain her excitement. Is there a dance party going on? She's down for it. An all-night movie marathon? She'll bring the popcorn. Zoey likes living life on the wild side!

Zuri

Zuri is a true city monkey. He loves living in the Marvelous Metropolis, especially when he gets to bring his buds to the zoo. He always brings extra snacks to share with the animals he visits.

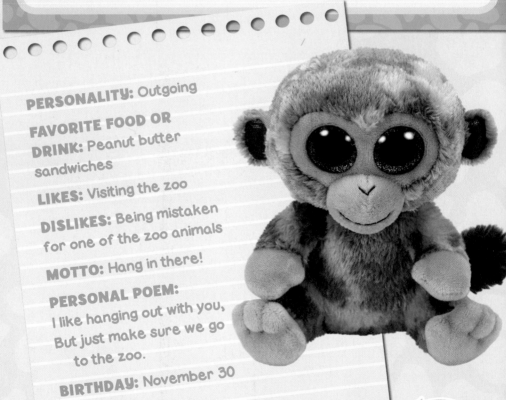

PERSONALITY: Outgoing

FAVORITE FOOD OR DRINK: Peanut butter sandwiches

LIKES: Visiting the zoo

DISLIKES: Being mistaken for one of the zoo animals

MOTTO: Hang in there!

PERSONAL POEM:
I like hanging out with you,
But just make sure we go
to the zoo.

BIRTHDAY: November 30

All About Me!